STAT$

NUMBERS TO KILL FOR

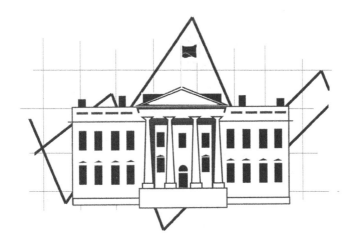

by MARK DONAHUE

DONAHUE
LITERARY PROPERTIES

STATS

ISBN-13: 978-1-7349711-2-5 (Paperback)

This is a work of fiction. The characters, incidents and dialogue are products of the author's imagination, any resemblance to actual persons, living or dead, is entirely coincidental. Any references to historical events, real people, or real places are used fictitiously.

Front cover design by Marsha Donahue. Illustration by Mary Susan Oleson, bludesignconcepts.net

Published in the United States of America by
Donahue Literary Properties, LLC.
www.DonahueLiteraryProperties.com

Dedicated to
All Navy Seals who keep us safe from the bad guys.

ACKNOWLEDGEMENT

HISTORY TEACHERS TELL US "PAST is Prologue" and "He who ignores the past is doomed to repeat it." History teachers know stuff. But their knowledge is based on what they read. They weren't there. Here is to all the history teachers who do more than read. To those who investigate, visit, challenge, push back, and defy the books in order to find the real history.

"I never thought I'd say this, but I miss voter fraud."
Jon Stewart

CHAPTER 1

Iraq, Desert, April 2009

THE BLACKHAWK MH-X HOVERED virtually unheard two hundred feet above and one mile south of its objective. The green images seen through night vision goggles by its Navy pilots made the objective appear like a glowing Christmas tree in the drab desert terrain.

In the back of the Blackhawk, a heavily armed combined squad of Navy Special Ops and SEAL Team 3 members sat placidly while they inhaled Jet A fuel fumes that mixed with the intoxicating aroma of spent gun powder. The unmistakable odor of human sweat also wafted through the back of the chopper. The pungent, nervous kind.

All eight stared straight ahead and awaited word from the pilots to initiate their well-rehearsed and meticulously planned operation. As the chopper hummed through the pre-dawn darkness, there were no thoughts of home or family in the minds of the squad. All thoughts were on the mission. Anything else would be a dereliction of duty, and duty mattered.

The yellow-pink glow in the eastern sky foretold of sunrise only minutes away. If weeks of reconnaissance proved accurate and schedules kept, the captives within the objective would be taken outside by their six guards just after dawn to use the crude bathroom facilities dug into the dirt. The two men would then be doused with cold well water from wooden buckets that would serve as their weekly shower.

Near the back of the chopper, one of the SEALs chewed several pieces of Juicy Fruit gum, the man next to him moved his leg up and down like a piston, a third had a tight grin on his face in anticipation of what was to come.

The team's goal was straightforward; rescue the two American congressmen who had survived an IED attack on their convoy before those same legislators were publicly executed by their relatively unknown but particularly vicious Islamic captors.

The congressmen had been on a fact-finding mission in Iraq to determine the "truth" about America's continued involvement in the never-ending war and a requested increase in financial resources to further the effort. Among the many truths they discovered was that Iraq was a dangerous place to be. The men had been taken hostage weeks earlier and held for ransom by a splinter group made up of a dangerous melding of Syrian, Iraqi, and Afghani forces. By policy, America would not pay a ransom.

Undeterred, the group had eagerly, with production quality rivaling a professionally produced McDonald's TV commercial, posted videos of the capture of the two congressmen and promised they would be placed in metal cages, have gasoline poured on them, and then lit to be burned alive in HD living color for all the world to see.

The sight and sound of the infidels being consumed in flames would serve as important propaganda fodder for the group in their world-wide recruiting efforts. The event would also serve notice to other American forces, politicians, and journalists as to what their fate would be if captured by the radicals. The online video event was scheduled to be broadcast within the next twenty-four hours.

Seven minutes after sunrise, a grainy satellite image of the two captured Americans and six guards in the Islamic compound appeared on the computer screen on the Blackhawk's control panel. The chopper crew removed their night vision goggles and now relied on what they could see in real time on their screens and out their windows.

The two naked congressmen had their hands and ankles tied with nylon bands as they shuffled through the dirt to the toilet holes under the control of six armed guards. They were twenty yards outside a group of block buildings that served as a holding location.

"We have a visual," the pilot said. "We're moving in. Descending to thirty feet. A.O., you hang back in case things go to shit."

"Roger that," A.O. replied.

As the chopper descended, the rest of the team prepared to exit using braided ropes that were tossed out the sliding doors of the Blackhawk. "Go," the pilot said.

Within eight seconds, the team of seven had exited the chopper and sprinted toward the largest of the buildings that was enclosed behind a ten-foot-high chain link fence topped with razor wire. The plan called for the good guys to surround the perimeter of the buildings in groups of three and four and use wire cutters to silently gain access to the complex.

Once inside, they would surprise and then eliminate the Islamic guards as they ate their breakfast. After the guards were neutralized, the good guys would find and extricate the congressmen, board the chopper, and return to base before seven a.m. It was a simple and logical plan prepared by the best military minds on the planet.

The plan went to shit.

Instead of having breakfast inside like they were supposed to, the six guards remained scattered on the outside of the four small buildings. They had concluded it would be far more entertaining to beat the hell out of the two congressmen for a while before their morning meal. The beating would not be for the purpose of gathering information or as punishment, but instead, just for fun. Something to get the day off to a rousing start.

The congressman from South Florida was led blindfolded to the center of a dirt enclosure, forced to his knees, and told to put his forehead on the dirt. Three laughing guards then took turns each kicking him in the head like it was a soccer ball. In Arabic, one of the men yelled "Goal!" after a particularly savage blow that left the congressman unconscious. The other men laughed at the witty football reference.

The second congressman from Ohio had been tied to a metal post in the yard while the three other guards took turns lashing him with belts that left over a dozen deep red gashes in his skin.

As the six Islamic guards continued their pre-breakfast entertainment in two different locations within the dirt enclosure, the seven American forces who had entered the compound were out of visual range of what was happening to the congressmen inside the small courtyard hidden amongst the four block buildings.

Once the chopper pilots could see via the satellite images what was happening to the congressmen, they immediately radioed for the ground forces to move quickly toward the area where the beatings were taking place.

The plan suddenly got far more problematic when an additional five armed guards— *not* part of the plan—rushed out of one of the buildings after they had spotted the American intruders inside the fence line. They immediately fired on the seven American troops who had come together as a group after they had entered the complex and were now pinned behind a low stone wall.

"Fuck, we have a shitstorm brewing down there. They have more guards than we thought" the co-pilot said. "A.O., you locked and loaded?"

"Roger that."

"We're gonna move in. Can you get a visual?"

A.O. looked through the scope and saw the targets. "Do a ninety and keep it steady."

"Coming around."

As the chopper moved into position, the three football-playing guards, seeing the situation that was unfolding in front of them, ran toward the tied-up congressmen brandishing swords. Their intent was to behead both men and save their heads and maintain at least part of their planned home video presentation.

As the first Islamic guard neared the helpless Ohio representative with his sword already raised, he was flattened by two bullets to his chest creating two resounding *whomps*.

This turn of events caused the remaining two sword-bearers to turn toward the chopper and gape in what ended up being fatal curiosity.

That made it easy. *Whomp- whomp, whomp- whomp.*

Having seen their three comrades fall, the three remaining belt-wielding guards in the courtyard grabbed their rifles and turned their full attention to the hovering chopper that was now within hearing distance only a quarter mile away. They knelt and opened fire on the chopper causing metallic pings to be heard inside the heavily armored Blackhawk.

The flashes from their weapons were like beacons to A.O. who homed in on the shooters with radar-like efficiency. Three single rapid-fire headshots did the job. *Whomp, whomp, whomp.*

The second group of five fighters fired at the chopper while continuing to hold the seven Americans who remained pinned behind the low concrete wall that was becoming lower and thinner with each rifle blast by the insurgents.

"We're taking incoming. Need to back away," the pilot said.

"Copy," A.O. said. "Just keep it level."

As the chopper moved higher and further from harm's way, A.O. identified what looked like the leader of the group of five that was holding down seven good guys.

A.O. didn't have to remember training. It was all reaction and muscle-memory now. The kinds of actions that had been imbedded over a period of years by screaming sergeants and endless drills. It was all reflex and execution. *Just do the fucking job like you're trained to do.* Sight the damn target through the scope. *Focus. Exhale. Ease back the trigger.* Two quick pulls, *whomp, whomp;* leader down, one to the head, one to the chest.

Next were the two short ones near the water well, *whomp-whomp, whomp- whomp,* then the tall one that tried to run away. Not fast enough—*whomp-whomp,* to the back. The last one was on his stomach taking careful aim at the Blackhawk. Too late. Two to his face made for a different sound, like water balloons hitting pavement.

All nineteen of A.O.'s trigger pulls found a target. Despite the higher altitude and distance, A.O. did not miss. Not once. After the five were eliminated in less than a minute, the seven American troops on the ground rose from behind the low wall, and within minutes, three of them had guided the naked Congressmen toward the chopper.

The remaining four went building by building and searched for more guards and to determine if there was any valuable intelligence inside the compound buildings. They found no more fighters, but took several notebooks, assorted files, and computer hard drives.

Before they left, they set several timed C-4 charges that would level the buildings soon after their departure. Within ten minutes all eight team members were safely on the chopper in the same "lucky" seats in which they had arrived. For some reason, the chopper smelled better on the return trip.

On the forty-minute ride back to base, there was little conversation except when the naked congressmen now covered with blankets kept thanking their rescuers. "We were dead men. Thank you, guys. We never knew it was like this. We never knew, I mean how could we know what you guys have to deal with?"

"You should thank A.O. over there," one of SEALs pointed out.

"Thank you, A.O. You saved our lives. That was unbelievable what you did," the congressman from Florida said emotionally.

"That sailor saved all our lives, Congressman, not just yours."

A.O. did not respond to the gratitude and instead stared out the window of the chopper at miles of endless brown desert and looked forward to breakfast.

CHAPTER 2

**Flagel and Schultz Econometric Forecasting, Inc., Manhattan
May 2012**

"HI MARSHA, HAVE A GOOD WEEKEND?"

"No," she replied and walked away without even a glance his way.

Dr. James McDowell, PhD, had seen her the first day she showed up at the office. She was kind of hard to miss. She possessed the body of doom and knew all eyes were on her when she walked through the office, even those of some of the other women.

Her name was Marsha, and she would be working in the office as a temp for a couple months replacing the redhead on maternity leave who had gotten knocked up by some guy in marketing after a company Christmas party the year before.

When Marsha walked through the office delivering mail or making copies, she made sure she emphasized her many assets that included impressive breasts, tiny waist, long legs, and ash blonde hair that was always tied up in a high schoolish ponytail. James really liked that high school ponytail and, on several occasions, tried to strike up a casual conversation with her, but she ignored what she saw as an older man. Much older.

But James was no quitter. He decided he would bide his time with Marsha and when the right opportunity arose, he would pounce like a cat, a tall middle-aged cat, and impress her with his numerous degrees and knowledge of all things numbers.

"Hey Marsha, did ya see the Yankees game last night?"

"I hate baseball."

Sure she may have walked away, but James thought she may have actually glanced at him. He felt that was real progress toward a potential meaningful relationship since he hated baseball too.

The day she had stood at the printer for nearly an hour and made all those copies, she had worn a short skirt, and she kept bending over as she retrieved the copies. Each time she did, she almost showed James the promised land. Was that a planned performance or was it just an accident? Did she know what she was doing? Could she tell that James was in a perfect position at his cube twenty feet from her to see what no one else could see?

After Marsha's copy machine presentation, James had a question as she passed his desk. "Hey Marsha, you want anything from Panera?"

"I hate Panera, their food sucks."

"Yeah me too but it's quick and I…"

Marsha walked away from James with several copies of documents marked "Confidential" and delivered them to senior management on the top floor of the office tower.

It was at that precise moment that others would have considered his efforts an unadulterated and even embarrassing failure. But James, instead, finally saw his opening and a path to ultimate success. He noticed Marsha had absentmindedly left the original document in the copier, and after she entered the elevator, he retrieved the papers and slid them into his briefcase.

In just minutes his agile brain had formulated an absolutely *foolproof plan*. He would hold onto the document overnight. The next day just before lunch, he would go to her desk and ask her if she had lost an original document at the copy machine.

She would of course confirm she had, and he would say "Oh, I think I have it. It must've gotten mixed up with stuff I copied." That of course would lead to some small talk, and then he would obviously invite her to lunch, where they would laugh and talk about stuff and then he would ask her if she had seen *Beautiful* on Broadway?"

"No," she would say.

"Oh, I have two tickets for Saturday night, wanna go?"

And of course she would say, "Cool, I'd love to go."

Then they'd go to the play and during the second act she would slide her right arm under his left arm and strategically position her ample right breast just below his triceps. He would act like he couldn't feel it, but he could feel it and she would know he could feel it.

After the play they would go to his apartment and after a little too much wine, they'd start making out and then she'd jump up and do a slow sensuous striptease just to get both of them in the mood. Then after a twenty-minute blowjob (maybe it would only be fifteen), she would screw his brains out because she couldn't help herself. Afterward, they would lie in bed, talk into the wee hours, and discuss their next date.

It was a great plan.

Then James read the document from the copier.

CHAPTER 3

JAMES HAD ALWAYS BEEN GOOD WITH numbers, and the numbers he was seeing in the eight-page document he had swiped from the copy machine, made no sense. At first he thought it was all a mistake, maybe just some typos, but these were no typos. It was simple math, and the math didn't add up.

As he read, he realized he had never seen this kind of statistical detail before. When he saw his name was not on the distribution list at the top of the memo, he almost decided to give it back to Marsha since it would have given him an excuse to begin the execution of "the plan."

But the document was interesting, maybe even more interesting than an evening with Marsha.

Right before midnight, as he sat up in bed reading, with his medium haired tuxedo cat named Rocky purring on his lap, he was for the first time able to see the data from all the other nine regional managers, a total group of ten of which he was a part. He saw the conclusions of that data that had been prepared from the reports. But it was clear as day to James that the combined figures should have led to a different number.

"Math doesn't lie," was a favorite saying of James' that he tried to bring into every conversation with young professional women in Soho bars to let them know he was indeed a math wizard. But the numbers in this memo had indeed lied.

What he had read led James to become annoyed, and well, just pissed off. Why was he doing all this work, all this research, only to have it ignored? "What the hell is going on?" he asked himself out loud. Rocky trilled in response.

The next morning at his cubicle, James kept rechecking the numbers he had read the night before and his pissed-off quotient continued to rise. He was ready to ask that *what the hell is going on* question to someone else besides Rocky, but no one was around.

The fact was, no one was ever around James since he worked virtually alone in an office cubicle in a place that other office workers called Nerd Isolation. His desk was surrounded by stacks of books on statistics and piles of reports that formed a kind of paper barrier and prevented anyone who would want to come back and shoot the breeze with James from doing so.

But truth be told, no one ever really wanted to shoot the breeze with James. More truth be told, James was not a great conversationalist unless someone wanted to talk about the beauty of linear equations.

After getting his doctorate from Princeton in statistics, where he also earned the nickname "Slim Jim," James decided to find work in Manhattan. He enjoyed museums, off-Broadway plays, and reading. In his mind, his current job was a placeholder until NASA finally replied to his many applications. So, as he waited for the phone to ring, he kept his head down, his mouth shut, and collected a nice paycheck.

So, before doing or saying anything rash about what he had discovered in the file, which was not James' way of doing things, he did several weeks of after-hours research on the work his firm had been conducting for decades.

After he made sure he could cover his computer hacking tracks, he accessed the emails and correspondence of everyone in his firm and analyzed other company historical records, including the reports they had prepared for nearly six decades. The more research he did, the more convinced he became that something wasn't right and hadn't been right for a long time.

As the information he had uncovered over the month piled up and simmered in his high-octane brain, he decided he was now definitely pissed off. He also felt a bit used, forgotten, and taken advantage of. He was fully aware how the numbers he had discovered could impact the country and maybe even the world.

He remembered a scene in a movie when the guy said, 'I'm mad as hell and I'm not going to take it anymore." He had forgotten what movie that was from, but that scene was how he felt.

James decided it was time to do something with the information he had uncovered. Time for him to make a big impression with the bosses on the top floor. He decided he would march right upstairs and tell his boss there had been a big mistake. The numbers were bogus. Someone had messed up big time. He would also tell his bosses that the company might get in some big trouble if other people found out the numbers that James had discovered were not accurate and maybe even fraudulent.

He concluded that such an aggressive and professional approach, based on his solid research—except for that hacking business into personal emails—might even warrant a raise or a promotion. Maybe both. He was totally psyched.

CHAPTER 4

"THERE HAS BEEN A BIG MISTAKE. These numbers are bogus, and you guys might get in some big trouble if people found out that what has been released is not accurate, and maybe even fraudulent."

What had sounded like a good way to start the conversation with his boss and his boss's boss when he was rehearsing it in front of his bathroom mirror earlier that morning, did not come out exactly the way James had hoped. In fact, it had inadvertently come out as a sort of a threat. After making his statement, he felt several moments of uncomfortable silence.

"First of all, James, I am surprised and disappointed that you would have read an internal company memo that was not addressed to you." James' boss, Stephan Flagel, said.

"How could I know it wasn't addressed to me until I started reading it?"

Ignoring the logic of a math guy, Stephan said, "As to the memo itself, I can understand your confusion, but you were only seeing part of the picture. We also use several independent sources to arrive at our final conclusions."

"That's clearly not what the memo said. It said you guys were going to simply lower the figure arbitrarily and release a made-up number that had nothing to do with the results of my work, the work of the other regional managers, our outside sources. That's not right, the numbers don't lie." James stated flatly.

James' boss's boss, a woman who was the owner of the firm, said nothing as she sat passively and listened to the conversation between the two men.

After several more exchanges, Stephan said, "James, thank you for bringing this issue to our attention. We will take it under advisement. You can go back to your office now."

"I don't have an office; I have a cube."

"Then please return to it. Now."

"But...these numbers they are, you know, bogus."

After several more moments of awkward silence, Stephan said, "James, I think it best given your disagreement with our processes and procedures, that you seek employment elsewhere."

"What? You mean I'm fired? I'm not getting a raise or a promotion?"

"You will get a ninety-day severance."

Back at his cubicle, a large security guard stood nearby and said, "You know you can't take no files with you."

"Yeah, I know the damn rules," James said. As he spoke, he opened his top drawer and slipped a red 256gb flash drive into his palm.

CHAPTER 5

Jefferson Market Branch, NYC Public Library, West Village
May 2012

"HEY MISTER, WAKE UP." INSTEAD of waking up, dark-haired, green-eyed, clean-cut, Ryan Reynolds-esque looking, NYU sweatshirt clad, blue jean-wearing, part-time cab driving, unpublished thirty-six-year-old David Dawson continued to snore.

The annoying sound echoed off the interior block walls of the hundred-year-old building. "C'mon man, we're closing this section and you can't stay here all night" the janitor, with mop in hand, pleaded.

David lifted his head off the oak table and with it drug a string of drool from a small pool of spit he had deposited on the loose-leaf binder he had used as a pillow. He awoke with a look of fear on his face. He knew he was somewhere but at that exact moment had no idea where the hell that somewhere was. Or when it was. He just knew he was late for something. "What time is it?" he blurted, afraid of what the answer might be.

"Little past eight."

"Oh, shit."

After David wiped away the drool on his sleeve, put on his blue steel rimmed glasses and Mets baseball hat, grabbed his notebook his laptop, and *Roget's Desk Thesaurus*-the tools to help him write the Great American Novel---he ran for the library door.

He bounded out onto Sixth Avenue then broke into a serious jog onto Tenth Street. He slowly increased his pace and hoped his late arrival would not mess up an evening that had significant potential on many levels.

When he stopped at the front door of the second floor walk-up apartment to catch his breath, he could hear Michael Bublé music through the door and detected the aroma of fresh baked Italian bread that wafted from inside. After he silently entered the apartment, he could see into the dining room where two bottles of merlot and four lit candles portended that the evening had in fact even more potential than he dared hope for. And he dared hope for a lot.

When he entered the kitchen, he saw Sydney, a trim dark-haired woman in her early thirties. She wore black leggings under a short plaid skirt, high heel boots, and a royal blue form-fitting off-the-shoulder top.

Humming an Adele tune, Sydney stood at the stove and stirred the homemade vegetable soup she had prepared the day before. She figured it was a perfect match for the lasagna she had picked up at the corner deli knowing it was a fan favorite and that tonight could be a very special occasion.

Silently sidling up from behind the unsuspecting woman, David put his arms around her waist and began nibbling at her neck. At first Sydney ignored her assailant then gave in to curiosity. "Who are you and what are your intentions?" Sydney calmly asked in between barely perceptible moans.

"Vile, repugnant, immoral, perverted, and in the eyes of many, shocking intentions."

"Oh, yummie. I was afraid you might be one of those run-of-the-mill type perverts. You know, no imagination or dedication to purpose. But we better hurry, my husband will be home soon."

"Why are you still married to that low-life unpublished loser?"

"He's better than nothing. C'mon, we need to get on with it. How about right here on the kitchen floor?"

"You know I love your body, but could I have some of that soup first?"

"It's me or the soup. Not enough time for both, and don't forget my husband may not be much to look at, but he's really strong and crazy jealous."

Lifting Sydney's skirt, David suggested, "Hmm, let's get creative here, you could feed me the soup while I'm…"

"You're a pig."

"Why, thank ya ma'am." David said with a remarkably bad John Wayne imitation.

Without turning around, Sydney pushed David's hand away, but he grabbed her, spun her around, put his arms around her waist and said, "Aha, I've caught you! It's me! Your loving, faithful, decidedly unattractive, jobless husband. And just who the hell is this guy you were going to do on our kitchen floor?"

Looking up at David with large brown eyes and an innocent smile on her face, Sydney asked, "Do you expect me to remember the name of every guy who comes around here when you're at the library all day? By the way, Steinbeck, you're late."

"Was working on a killer paragraph that could change the world as we know it and…"

"Save it, I put the lasagna in an hour later than usual. I know you by now."

David smiled, smacked Sydney on the butt, then grabbed an apple from the bowl on the counter and took a noisy bite. "So, how was work?" he asked.

"Boring."

"Did you really think being a CPA would be a career filled with excitement and cheap thrills?"

"I know it's part-time until you're on the best-seller list, so I can handle the boredom for a while. Besides, it pays the bills. Some of them anyway."

"Did you hear anything about that gig at the Pentagon?"

"Not yet. I think it might be a few more weeks. Hope we don't run out of food in the meantime."

"Yeah, but doesn't looming financial ruin and starvation add an element of risk to our sex lives?"

"Hmm, multiple orgasms or money in the bank? Tough call."

"If my agent does her job, maybe we'll have both. She told me four publishers really liked what they read. I think I'll hear something by..."

"Have you checked your email in the last hour?"

"No."

"Maybe you should" Sydney said with a smile as she handed David her iPad so he could see there was an email from his agent.

David gawked at the highly anticipated message from Smithson Literary Agents and could see on the subject line "Publisher Responses." The smile that had been on his face seconds before quickly disappeared. He stared at the tablet's screen for several moments but instinctively backed away when Sydney handed it to him. "Here, go on and open it." She said.

Instead, David moved to the kitchen window and stared out into the late spring evening. "This is like when you buy a Powerball ticket and the prize is a gazillion dollars. Until they draw the number and you realize you've lost, you always have that hope. Always have the dream."

Sydney walked up behind David and put her head against his back and her arms around his shoulders. "Honey, I know this has been tough, but you said yourself how much everyone liked this one. Your agent said this was your best yet."

"Liking and publishing are two different things."

"Want me to open it?"

"Sure, why not? Maybe it will change our luck."

With David's back to her, Sydney sat the iPad on the kitchen counter, opened the email, and read it. She had no expression on her face when David turned and looked at her. She whispered a simple, "No."

"All four said no?" David said in a hoarse voice.

Sydney nodded.

Suddenly exuding some false bravado, David smiled, took the iPad from Sydney, hit "print", and the printer on the kitchen desk spat out the copies of the four "Sorry, it's not for us" responses from the publishers.

David took the copies and placed them in a desk drawer that contained dozens of other rejection letters. "Well, as that famous philosopher Ellen DeGeneres once said, 'It's failure that gives you the proper perspective on success.' Based on that concept, my perspective is going to be 20/20."

David turned back to the window and watched the muted luster of a Manhattan lit sky turn from purple to dark blue. After a few moments he said, "Maybe I should finish my master's and go teach somewhere. Or go back to the Navy. I can't really drive a cab forever."

"You go back, and I go back. You'd hate teaching, and I'd hate you if you went back to doing what you were doing before. Everyone says it's tough getting started as a writer. You have to stick with it. Besides, you know you're good. I know you're good."

David remained silent for several moments. "How about going to a ballgame tomorrow night?"

Tears formed in Sydney's eyes as she moved next to David and looked out into a moonless Manhattan night. "Sure, but you know the Mets suck."

CHAPTER 6

THE NEXT MORNING DAVID TOOK out his literary frustrations on the heavy bag at his musty gym, a place in Brooklyn with no name on it. The gym had opened sometime during the Wilson administration and had apparently avoided any paint or other renovations since that time.

The more David thought about all the rejection notices piling up in his desk drawer, the madder he got and the harder he hit.

He threw scores of jabs, upper cuts, roundhouse crosses, as sweat rolled down his face and chest. His trim, chiseled body glistened in the yellow half-light of the gym that smelled a bit like an old sweaty basketball shoe that had been sprayed with weak disinfectant. It didn't smell awful, but it still smelled.

After seven minutes of beating the hell out of the defenseless canvas bag, a large, heavily tattooed young man leaning against a pole asked. "Hey old man, you just beat up bags or do wanna to spar a little?"

First of all, the guy was pretty damn big. Second, he had some tattoos that indicated he liked to beat people to death. Those two items alone in David's mind were reasons enough to say, "No thanks, just getting ready to leave."

"C'mon, old man, no head shots just some body work, you know a little workout. I won't hurt ya."

"Nah, I need to get going and…"

"Hey man, you a pussy or what?"

David decided he did not like that guy. "What's your name, tiger?"

"José."

"Okay, José, just a couple rounds and no head shots, right?" José nodded and smiled.

After the men climbed into the ring and touched gloves, José immediately threw a left hook to the side of David's head that knocked him on his butt. After shaking his head several times trying to get his bearings David said, "Hey asshole, I thought you said no headshots."

"My bad, man. Guess I forgot."

At that point, David knew for sure he did not like José. He got on his feet and looked up at the six foot five, 230 pounds, twenty-three-year-old, and decided this had been a big mistake. At the same time, he also knew that given proper boxing gym etiquette, decorum, and reputation, it was too late to back out now.

As the two men slowly circled each other in the ring, they threw out pawing left jabs trying to find an opening. Other boxers began to gather around outside the ring to see some action between the big tough looking tattooed Hispanic dude and the slender metrosexual looking green-eyed, white guy. They smelled blood, and it wasn't Latin blood.

José threw a soft left jab at David then quickly followed that up with a vicious right hand cross that, if it had connected , would have ended the match quickly. But David deftly ducked under the punch and fired a left uppercut into José's ribs. The "ummph" sound José made belied the forced smile on his face. The punch hurt, and David knew it hurt. Most importantly, José knew that David knew it hurt.

Showing more power than skill, José unloaded with back-to-back combinations in an apparent effort to remove David's head from his shoulders. David caught the punches with his gloves and used his quickness to circle out of harm's way. *The man can punch,* David thought.

The big man began to stalk David around the ring like prey. Using angles, he tried to force him to move into a corner where he could overwhelm him with a series of powerful head and body shots.

But David was too quick, and every time José got close, David would pepper him with a flurry of jabs then easily move away from him. At first, those jabs were just minor annoyances to José. But as David realized he was much quicker than the big guy, he began to put more power behind his jabs, leaving angry crimson marks all over José's face.

David could hear José's breathing become more and more labored as he tried to corner him. He could also see that José dropped his left hand every time he threw a right hand punch. David began to time those punches and waited.

Near the end of the four-minute round, José got frustrated that he couldn't land a solid punch or stop David's rapid-fire hammer-like left jabs that had drawn blood from his nose and mouth and opened up a sizable cut above his right eye.

José wanted the match to end ASAP, so he loaded up a right cross and threw everything he had at David's head. Unfortunately for José, he also dropped his left hand again, exposing his left jaw. It was an easy target for the right uppercut David had been saving.

José saw the punch coming. But it was too late to do anything about it since he was off balance, tired, and wished at that moment there weren't about forty guys standing around the ring who were going to see what would happen next.

When David's punch landed, José's head snapped backward, and he began to back pedal across the ring. When he hit the ropes with his shoulders, he sprang forward, and David caught him in the solar plexus with a left uppercut that emptied José's lungs right before the big man fell face forward onto the mat with a sound that was eerily close to a "splat."

Hershel, the black seventy-seven-year-old trainer at the gym, came up to David as he left the ring and said, with what could be considered a legitimate giggle, "I tried to tell that big ol' boy not to go messin' with you. But he said you was just a skinny white dude who writes books."

David laughed and said, "Well, Hershel, if you hadn't taught me that left uppercut, things might have been different in there."

Hershel laughed and said, "Bet that big ol' boy won't mess with you no more. That there was a beautiful thing to see."

David waved good-bye to Hershel and left the gym to go for a jog as José finally reached a sitting position in the ring where he stayed until he was sure David had left the building.

When David returned to his apartment, he was met with three more email rejection notices from his agent, all of which he dutifully printed and added to his collection. He also found a separate letter from his agent that said she was firing him. She also suggested he may want to try banking as a new career.

Except for his uplifting encounter with José, the day had been a total disaster.

CHAPTER 7

OVER THE NEXT SEVERAL MONTHS, David wrote every day. He tried all the genres—mystery, adventure, science fiction, even comedy, but he just didn't feel very funny at the time. He tried novels, novellas, novelettes, short stories, even op-eds for newspapers, but no one responded. David hid the rejections so Sydney wouldn't find them.

He made a point of not complaining to Syd or having her suspect he was feeling sorry for himself, even though he was, sure as hell, feeling sorry for himself. He would take breaks from his writing and go to the gym, jog through Central Park, or spend time in the library either reading other writers trying to discover what they had that he didn't or doing research on his latest project.

He thought about taking a break from the writing to clear his head but felt he would be cheating Syd if he did. He feared she would suspect he was losing his focus. He didn't want that. So, he just kept writing, sort of like when Forrest Gump just kept running.

His failure as a writer was having a negative impact on David on many levels. He had never failed before and discovered he was not good at the failure thing. At the same time, he was not the kind of guy who gave up either. He had proven that many times in his life as well. He figured he just needed a break. He needed to come up with an idea that would allow him to display his writing skill, his flair for character development, plot twists, and killer endings.

If King, Grisham, Patterson, and the rest of those guys could come up with stories, he figured it was just a matter of time before he could dream up a story too. That's all he needed; just one damn good story. Until he did, he would keep writing every day. *Every* day.

CHAPTER 8

Pegasus Publishing, NYC, Ten months later

ON HIS ARRIVAL AT PEGASUS that afternoon, David was, by anyone's reasonable observation, a total mess. He wore dirty ripped jeans, a dingy Mets cap, and his sweat stained Jets jacket were all testimony to his twenty-minute jog/limp from his apartment to the East 44th Street art deco-style office building.

He had a nasty bruise on the left side of his face, and a deep scrape that was already starting to scab over that ran from his cheek bone to his chin. The rest of his face and both hands were scratched with numerous visible traces of dried blood and nasty gouges.

He carried with him a manila file filled with a manuscript of sorts. Papers were haphazardly piled and stuck out of the file in all directions. It appeared David had successfully avoided a shave, shower and meaningful sleep for several days.

His head and back were killing him. He was so tired that he nodded off a few times as he sat in the small, hot waiting room that had a cacophony of odors emanating from a thirty-year-old carpet and even older red cloth-covered chairs that were worn and stained at the same time.

On their website, Pegasus defined themselves as a "multi-genre publisher, not bound by normal publishing limitations." They also advertised that they looked for talented and previously unpublished authors whom they could "nurture and grow with."

They were known for publishing weird conspiracy theory stuff that actually sold and made money for the company and their authors. Of course more traditional and respected publishers considered Pegasus just above the *National Enquirer* or *The Star*. But those big publishers conceded that the company had developed an audience who never tired of reading about alien abductions or latest detailed sightings of an aging Elvis on a beach in Rio.

That all sounded good to David. He needed someone, *anyone*, to take a chance on him and his story. To believe him. Even if his story *was* fucking crazy. Of course at that point a guy with a printing press in his garage whose part-time stripper girlfriend moonlighted as his editor would also have sounded pretty good to David.

Pegasus was also the only publisher that would agree to meet him without being represented by an agent, and that aspect alone added a great deal of allure for him since he had not been able to find a new agent in almost a year.

Maybe Pegasus was just the right spot for him. A place he would eventually call home. His writing home. Or maybe not.

But in his mind he had moved far beyond just the issue of being published. He had a story to tell, and it was extremely important that someone listened to him. It was more than important; it was vital.

He recognized the importance of his story and what he had come to know over the previous ten months. At times he could hardly believe what he had seen and learned. It was something he would have never thought possible.

Based on what he had learned, he had concluded that for the good of the country, he had to take aggressive action to do whatever needed to be done. Just like when he was on a mission in the Navy. He wasn't quite sure what that aggressive action was, but he was working on it.

Seven other visitors in the waiting room looked at him with suspicion, disdain or maybe fear. Some held their neatly bound works of literary art in their laps, looking for a publisher. Others were looking for jobs and held resumes. Still others were agents ready to pitch the editors at Pegasus. No matter who they were and what they did, they could all sense David was different from them. He *was* different from them now. Far more different than he had been ten months earlier or even forty-eight hours earlier.

CHAPTER 9

DAVID COULD SEE WHY THE other people in the office looked at him like he was a bit off after he glanced at his reflection in the glass door when he walked in. He looked like shit, and maybe a little crazy. He concluded that wasn't all bad. At least he had their attention, and he could, if need be, do crazy better than most.

He had already been waiting for nearly an hour and as the minutes dragged on beyond his appointment time, his fatigue worsened. He became more impatient and agitated as his physical and mental exhaustion battled the two Red Bulls he had swigged before arriving at Pegasus.

His left knee began to move up and down like a piston. Sweat beaded up on his brow, and his eyes darted nervously from person to person in the waiting room, all of whom did their best to avoid direct eye contact with a guy who clearly had issues.

After another half hour, David decided that given the fact he possessed information that could impact the world and that someone might walk in that office at any minute and try to kill him, he needed to act. "Miss, I had an appointment at 1:30. It's nearly 3."

"Mr. Marshall will be with you as soon as he can; he is very busy today, sir," the receptionist said without looking up from her cell phone and the series of texts she was getting from her BFF regarding the date she had gone on the night before with the *hottest guy ever.*

"Mr. Marshall should learn to keep his damn appointments. I was here on time, where the hell was he?"

"Sir, if you'd like to leave your manuscript, he'll get back to you if there's interest."

"Oh, there'll be interest alright, if he ever decides to make our meeting. Did you tell him I was here, Miss?"

"He knows you're here, it won't be long, sir. Thank you for being patient."

"Who said I was being patient? I'm not being patient at all," David knew it would in fact be long, and he also knew time was running out.

He began to tap his foot, which seemed to gain speed as the minutes ticked past. The others in the waiting room became more uncomfortable with what they saw as a combustible situation regarding the nervous, dirty, sweaty, beat-up guy with a stack of papers in his arms. One reed-thin writer of a children's coloring book decided to come back to Pegasus on another day and left.

After David began talking to himself, a second man, who had come to Pegasus with the idea of a story about cloning Michael Jackson's DNA and becoming his manager, decided David looked too crazy for him and also left.

Given the dwindling waiting-room population, David decided it was time.

CHAPTER 10

AFTER SEVERAL MORE MINUTES, DAVID said to no one in particular, "Damn editors and publishers are all alike. They can't write so they pretend they know how to read. They're all fucking assholes."

"Sir, I have to ask you to keep your profane comments to yourself or I'll be forced to call security," the receptionist said after she finally tore herself away from her Facebook page and actually looked at David.

"Here's a riddle, folks: Know how you can tell if an editor is an asshole? They hire brain-dead idiots for receptionists," David pointed out. "Get it?"

"Sir, I must ask you to leave now."

"Fuck you! I've had this appointment for almost a week and have been sitting here nearly two hours waiting. Go tell your boss I can make him a million dollars if he just gets his ass out here."

Brianna, the receptionist, picked up her phone, covered the mouthpiece with her hand, and whispered into it. Less than a minute later, a preppy, slender man stepped into the waiting room.

Andover-and Yale-educated Jonathan Robert Marshall was a thirty-eight-year-old editor who had been waiting for Simon & Schuster to reach out to him at any minute and make him a senior editor. He was sure it would happen. Any day.

Based on that hope, he tried to make himself look forty-eight in an effort to appear more imposing and scholarly. He even wore horn-rimmed glasses despite the fact he had 20/20 vision. So far his tactics hadn't worked in luring Simon & Schuster.

"Mr. Dawson?"

"It's about damn time."

"Mr. Dawson, I understand you've been verbally abusive to Brianna. Therefore, I must ask you to leave immediately or…"

"Verbally abusive? What did I say?"

"Brianna, what did he say to you?"

"Well, he like, called me a brain-dead idiot and said editors, were… like, assholes."

"Facts are facts. Miss Genius here *is* a brain-dead idiot, and everyone knows editors *are* assholes. So what's the big deal?" David logically explained.

"Mr. Dawson, whatever you have written, I can say without equivocation, I have absolutely no interest in reading it. If you don't leave immediately, I'm going to call security."

"Bullshit. I'm not going anywhere. Not this time."

One of the five people who remained in the waiting room, seeing impending big trouble, stood and started for the door. When he did, David pulled a pistol and pointed it at the writer of a book that claimed unicorns were alive and living in the Brazilian jungle.

"Sit the fuck down, dickwad."

The dickwad returned to his seat, sat down, and along with everyone else in the room, stared at David in respectful silence.

"Mr. Dawson, please, there's no reason for all this…"

"No reason? You don't know my story and have the balls to say there's no reason? How the hell do you know? Maybe there's a damn good reason. Maybe the whole fucking country is at risk, and I'm trying to save it, and I have a bunch of people trying to kill me and my family because of my story. Would that be reason enough for all this?"

The room remained quiet as the small group of writers, job seekers, and agents representing stories about puppies, unicorns, the undead, and famous Nazis, along with Brianna and Jonathan, nervously stared at David. They collectively and individually wished they were anywhere else in the world than the Pegasus Publishing Company at that particular moment.

"How many people are back in those offices?" David asked when he pointed to the office area that Jonathan had just come from.

"No one's back there. Today's Friday; everybody left but me."

"Workaholic, huh, Jonathan? Is there a conference room back there?"

"Yes."

"Hey Genius, does Jon here have any more appointments today?"

After checking her appointment book, Brianna announced, "No."

"Okay, everybody get up and move back to the conference room now." David ordered.

The group was at first hesitant and stayed in their seats while they looked at each other. Then in unison, they placed their manuscripts, briefcases, or purses in front of them as if they were shields capable of protecting them from a bullet.

"I said get your butts up and follow Marshall here back to the conference room. You too, Miss Brianna, and all of you give me your cell phones."

The three women and two men rose as one and followed Jonathan and Brianna into the back of the office. As they filed into the conference room, David took everyone's cell then yanked the landline phone cord out of the wall. He shut the door and quickly moved back to the front door, locked it, and turned off the waiting-room light.

When he returned to the conference room, the seven literary types, including Brianna and Jonathan, stood around a large oak conference room table under a garish overhead light made of faux crystal. The décor was 1970's vintage. The chairs were an ugly faded orange, and many had cuts and tears in the plastic seat coverings. The table was littered with empty coffee cups, several half-drunk water bottles, and what looked like a box of two-day-old Dunkin' Donuts.

"Wow, figured you guys made lots of cash, but never thought you'd have all this." David said sarcastically.

David placed the folder with his unkempt manuscript on the table and motioned for everyone to sit. They did and looked at David warily.

"You all think I'm going to kill everybody, don't you? I don't really want to, but I guess that's up to you guys. All I really want you to do is to listen to my story because no one else will."

"We don't think you're going to kill all of us, David. Really, we don't. You seem like far too nice a man to do such an awful thing," the agent from Queens said with conviction.

After staring at the agent for a few moments, David said, "Maybe I'll just shoot you, you fucking suck-up. Now shut up."

After the agent shut up, David went on, "Look folks, I've gone to every agent and publisher in town, to all the networks, to the *National Enquirer*, called the White House, my congressman, even contacted Oprah, but everyone thinks I'm nuts."

Realizing the irony of that statement as he waved his pistol around, David added, "Okay all this may look like I'm nuts, but I'm really not. I'm just trying to save this country. Okay, that sounds nuts too, but I'm not nuts. I just don't know what else to do or where else to go."

David began moving around the conference room table as he spoke. He looked in the donut box and picked out a half-eaten bagel and began to gnaw on it. "Sorry, I haven't eaten much the last few days. Anybody want a donut?"

Getting no takers, David went on. "So after I was ignored by everyone, I decided to write a book about what I had learned and experienced but like I said, no agent or publisher would even read it. So what choice do I have? All I am trying to do is let this country know what's going on. I'm trying to save this country, do the right thing, and no one cares. What the hell am I supposed to do?"

The group sitting around the conference room table was in a quandary. Did the crazy guy with the gun just ask a rhetorical question? Or was it an actual question, and would he shoot them if they did not provide a reasonable answer? Finally, it was Jonathan who risked a bullet to his skull.

"Mr. Dawson, with all due respect…"

"Please, call me David."

"Okay, David, you're obviously upset about something and maybe rightly so, but waving that gun around is a bit disconcerting. We know you don't want to hurt anyone, but could you please put it down so it doesn't go off accidently?"

"Yeah I guess, but if anybody tries to leave, I may have to shoot them in the leg or something." David helpfully pointed out.

David put the gun down in front of him and sat at the head of the table, like the CEO of a small public company.

"Thank you, David. So, you said you wrote a story?" Jonathan asked.

"Yes, but no one believes it."

"I assume it is nonfiction?"

"That's correct."

"Would you like to tell us your story, David?"

"Obviously. Do you think I'd pull a gun and bring everybody back here if I didn't want to tell my damn story?"

"Of course, then go ahead, David, please tell us your story. Needless to say, you now have our undivided attention."

"Okay. Even before I left NYU, I'd been driving a cab to make ends meet while I tried to write a best seller. Anyway, one day last June I picked up a fare in Harlem out in front of Judi's on Seventh Avenue. It was raining like a bitch. He was a tall, thin, pale, nerd-like guy."

CHAPTER 11

Seventh Avenue out in front of Judi's, June 2012

DAVID SAT IN HIS CAB HALF asleep. He was clean-shaven, well-groomed, tired, and unpublished. The noise of the pouring rain pounding on the roof of his cab was loud and soothing at the same time. He hoped he wouldn't get another fare for a while so he could knock off early, get home to Syd, order in some pizza, and watch whatever was on AMC that night.

Within seconds of that idyllic thought, a tall, thin man stumbled out of a Kinko's into the downpour. He lugged two thick brown briefcases and clumsily clamored into the back seat of the first empty cab he saw, which happened to be David's. For a few seconds he seemed to gather himself before he announced, "I need to go to Washington, DC, right away."

"Mister, DC's three hours away. You're better off taking the train. I can take you to Penn Station if you like," David offered.

"I don't want to take a train. I want you to drive me there."

"I'm just ending my shift and have plans for tonight and I can't..."

"I'll give you a thousand dollars cash to drive me."

"For real?"

"For real."

"Let me see it."

The tall, thin man pulled out a large wad of cash and peeled off ten one hundred dollar bills and handed them to David.

"These real?"

"They're real."

"They feel real," David said, almost to himself.

"For God's sake, they *are* real. Can we get going?"

"Where to in D.C.?"

"Pennsylvania Avenue. I'll give you specific directions when we get closer."

"Alright, but I need to make a call..."

"No calls. You call anyone and the deal is off."

David looked in the rearview mirror, shrugged his shoulders, and put down his cell phone. "For a grand, I guess my wife will understand if I come home a little late. Does that include the tip?"

When the tall, thin man did not answer, David assumed the grand included the tip but he felt he had an obligation to ask.

The man in the back seat was James McDowell, PhD. He was forty-eight, single and really smart. He looked like a college professor, which he had been for twelve years before finding a job in the private sector. That job had paid very well until he had gotten fired the day before.

He wore a wrinkled sport coat that smelled of mint-flavored pipe tobacco. He of course wore horn rimmed glasses. He was wet from the rain and breathed heavily. He had two large briefcases with him, one on the seat next to him, the other on the floor between his legs.

After a few minutes, James slumped down in the seat, put his head back, and took several deep breaths. David saw what was happening.

"You okay, mister?"

"I'm fine. Can we make it there before five?"

"Depends on the traffic."

"I'll give you another hundred if we get there by 4:30."

David gunned the engine, and the cab sped up. He also sensed an opportunity. "How much for 4:00?"

James ignored David, put his head back, and closed his eyes.

"I was just kidding," David said softly, although he really wasn't kidding.

Forty minutes later David, utilizing his finely tuned New York City cab driver skills, negotiated onto I-95 and was headed south toward DC. As the cab moved into Jersey, the traffic finally thinned. From time to time, he looked in his rearview mirror and saw James staring out the window. He looked tired. Even exhausted. When his eyelids drooped, he would shake himself awake and seemed to instinctively grab onto the briefcases more tightly.

After an hour, David had an announcement. "Mister, I need to pee."

"How long will that take?"

"Never timed a piss before."

"Okay, but hurry. And leave your cell phone here."

"Hurry a piss? While I'm inside, you want a Coke or something? I'm buying."

"Just a bottled water please."

After David tossed his cell on the front seat and left the cab to take his untimed piss, James sank further down into the seat, closed his eyes, and dozed off. When David returned to the cab and opened the door a few minutes later, he startled James who awoke from his catnap in a semi-panic. "Wha...where are we? I need to..."

"Easy mister, it's just me. Here, I brought you a couple bottles of water."

James regained his composure and took the water from David. "Thank you, and please call me James. Sorry I'm a bit edgy but I haven't gotten much sleep recently. Guess it's catching up with me."

"No problem. I know from lack of sleep, been there."

Minutes later David pulled back onto I-95. "So, James, what takes you to DC?"

"A meeting."

"What do you do?"

"Until yesterday I worked for an econometric forecasting cooperative."

"You must have needed a big business card."

In the rearview mirror, David could see that James smiled briefly.

"What did you do at that place?"

"We tracked economic trends and provided statistical analysis of data for public and private sector groups."

"Sorry, but that stuff sounds boring as hell. I mean, do people really pay attention and actually pay for that stuff?"

"Some people pay very close attention and pay significant sums for such information."

"Really? Big cash in that kind of business?"

"For some."

After several miles of silence, David tried to change the subject. "Like baseball? The Mets suck this year."

"No, I don't like sports."

"Wow, no sports."

"Golf is intriguing, although I have never played it."

"Wow, no sports." David repeated, a bit of awe mixed with sadness in his voice.

James then took a stab at a conversation starter. "Do you follow politics?"

"Yeah, a little."

Encouraged by David's less than enthusiastic response, James scooted up to the edge of his seat and rested his arms on the back of the front seat of the cab. "What do you think of the election in November?"

"I don't know. No real differences are there? Nothing ever changes no matter who gets in."

"Maybe nothing actually gets done, but who gets in really does matter, in thousands of ways to millions of people."

"All that fighting and nothing ever gets done, except…ever notice how much money senators and congressmen make when they're in office? They're all millionaires. I wonder how that shit happens?" David asked.

"That's why it matters who gets elected. Billions, even trillions of dollars are at stake."

"Sounds like all of them are on the take."

"Most of them are, in one way or the other. It's not about issues or policies. It's all about sucking up to donors and being willing to say anything or support any cause, so a donor will write a big check." James explained.

"That's why I don't follow politics all that much. It looks and sounds like bullshit."

"Who are you voting for in November?"

"I'll vote for Obama again. He seems like a good guy. Smart and classy dude, too. Plus unemployment numbers are down since he took office."

"How do you know?"

"How do I know what?

"How do you know the unemployment numbers are down?" James asked as if he knew the answer to his own question.

"I read and watch TV…they all say things are better."

"But how do you know that what they say is true?"

"Like I said, I read, watch cable TV, listen to the radio, and they all say things are getting better."

Suddenly animated, James pushed the issue. "Yes. That's what they all say, but the fact is you don't really know things are getting better, do you? You *think* you know, but you don't *really* know. All you know is what you hear from some talking head on TV or hear on the radio. Ever wonder where they get their information? If the radio and TV guys say things are better and show some numbers that they say prove it, you just accept those numbers as fact. If they say things are going to shit, you believe that too, right?"

"Isn't that what everybody does?"

"Yes! Yes…that's exactly what everybody does."

CHAPTER 12

Offices of Flagel and Schultz Econometric Forecasting Services, Inc. Manhattan, June 2012

A YOUNG INTERN KNOCKED ON the door of Stephan Flagel, CEO of Flagel and Schultz. After receiving a "Yes, what is it?" response, he entered the glass-enclosed office.

"Mr. Flagel, I couldn't locate Dr. McDowell. His desk was cleared off as ordered, and his secretary said she thought he'd left town for the weekend."

"Did she know where he went?"

"No sir."

"Did you ask?"

"Yes sir."

"Did you try his cell?"

"Yes, and his home phone. I even texted him but got no response."

"Let me know if you hear from him."

"Yes sir."

After the intern left his office, Stephan chewed on his pen for a few moments, decided he better make the call, and dialed. "Connie, it's me, Stephan. No one has seen McDowell since late yesterday, even though he was supposed to come back today, sign some paperwork, and pick up his severance check from HR. I'm not saying we have to worry, but he was quite upset at what he saw and read, to say nothing of the termination."

On the other end of the line, Connie disagreed. "Of course we have to worry, Stephan. Especially after the performance James put on in yesterday's meeting. His ranting and raving was totally unacceptable. The man is clearly troubled. I believe, along with others on the board, that he is now a genuine threat to us."

"I doubt very seriously he is any kind of threat. Besides, he's never been part of any high-level discussions and…"

"Have you determined how he gained access to the memo in the first place?"

"The temp we had in that week accidently left the original memo in the copy machine, and James found it. As a result, he was able to see information that was not intended for his eyes. That memo contained statistical analysis that went back some time. It also appears he, or someone working with him, may have hacked into our computer system over the last several weeks and gained access to some sensitive email chains. He was very computer savvy."

"How far back do you think he looked?" Connie asked.

"Almost three years, but I don't think McDowell would...I mean he wouldn't..."

"If he hacked into our computer system, he did so for a reason. I think it is very likely he may have made copies of everything he saw. If he made copies, it is equally likely he intends to do something with that information that could cause us...embarrassment."

"I must admit there was an indication of someone downloading data from an off-campus site."

There was silence for several moments as Connie digested what Stephan had just said. "First of all, Stephan, I am very disappointed in your carelessness in this matter. It was not a temp's fault; it was your fault. Secondly, this is no time to take any chances. I'll take care of it because frankly, Stephan, I question whether or not you would or could."

"But Connie, he's been here for ten years, and he is not the type of person who would..."

"Stephan dear, you sound like a misguided, illusionary pussy. But don't worry, Connie will take care of it. Connie always takes care of it."

After Connie abruptly hung up, Stephan stared at the receiver in his hand for several seconds before finally returning it to its base. For several more seconds, he stared out at the Manhattan skyline and saw a leaden sky as it continued to disgorge a torrential rain. When he spun around in his chair, he grabbed the TV remote and flipped on CNN where host Wolf Blitzer interviewed Jake Tapper.

"Jake, how do these new unemployment numbers showing a four-year low of 7.8% impact the election?"

"Wolf, the numbers mean very simply that the economy is slowly getting better. More people are getting back to work and if that trend continues, Obama is going to be hard to beat."

"This is the fourth month in a row these numbers have gone down. How low do your sources indicate they could fall the rest of the year?"

"Given how the rate has fallen over the last few months, I've been told it could go as low as 6.7 to 6.5% and that will make it very tough on Romney. The American public is seeing progress, which is not good news for the Republicans."

Stephan flipped over to Fox News and saw Shepard Smith interview Republican strategist Richard Moore.

"Richard, it appears the White House has gotten more good economic news, given today's unemployment report."

"Well, we think those numbers are still way too high and that this so-called recovery is still far too slow and something Governor Romney will make much better when he is in office."

"C'mon Richard, I know the talking points, but isn't it clear that this report indicates that perhaps the president's policies are taking hold and the economy is finally recovering from the deepest recession in decades?"

"Shepard, we're still months away from an election and much can happen between now and then and..."

"Richard, in all candor, it sounds like you're hoping the economy goes back into the tank so it helps your candidate in November."

"I'm not saying that at all, I'm simply saying..."

Stephan clicked off the TV and returned to looking at the rain as it attempted but failed to cleanse Manhattan.

CHAPTER 13

Cab on I-95

"SO WHO ARE YOU VOTING for, James?"

"I'm not voting."

"Really?"

"Really."

"Why not?"

"It doesn't matter who I vote for or who you vote for."

"I know. But I just feel better when I vote. Like I'm part of something bigger than me. Really a part of the country, you know?" David said.

"I do know, but it's all been decided, which is why I don't vote, and you waste your time when you do."

"Decided? Election's not till November."

"Nothing can or will change the outcome. Like I said, it's all been decided"

"That's nuts. So who's gonna win?" David asked.

"Obama, by four points."

"If you knew that for sure, you should go to Atlantic City or Vegas and bet the house."

"Oh, I will. I most certainly will." James said, a grin on his face.

"How can you be so sure Obama will win five months out?"

"Because of millions of people just like you."

"Like me?"

"You believe everything you hear and read, and you also vote."

"What's wrong with that? I'm voting for Obama because of his foreign policy and because the economy is getting better. Aren't those reasons enough to vote for the guy?"

"What if the economy was really getting worse? What if unemployment was really much higher than you think it is?"

"But it's not, it's getting better."

"I hear what you're saying, but, what if it *wasn't* getting better? What would you do then?"

CHAPTER 14

IN LESS THAN THREE MINUTES, the two men in expensive dark blue business suits had defeated the locks and entered first Dr. McDowell's apartment building and then his unit. With military precision they opened drawers, lifted his mattress, checked his shower, emptied his food cabinets onto the floor, looked in his medicine chest and generally beat the hell out of everything that was not nailed down. If they didn't find anything, they at least wanted McDowell to know they were serious about finding something.

After ten minutes they were ready to file their report on a cell to their boss. "Nothing here but a train schedule."

"Where to?"

"It's for the Acela trains to Boston, Philly, and DC."

"Shit. Check his credit cards and see if he charged a ticket," the boss said.

After a minute of typing into his smartphone, one of the men in suits found something. "He charged a hotel room in DC. The Hay-Adams, for tonight. Also looks like he was on the internet to see if he could get a New York cab to take him to DC."

"Okay, grab the next train to Washington. Maybe he'll be on it. Look for him."

"Hey, just found something else here in his office. Looks like he made some notes on a talk he's giving to a group called C-Span, whatever that is. Looks like he's planning on giving some kind of presentation to them tomorrow morning at 9."

"Fuck me," the boss said. "Get your asses on that train."

"Got it. We should be in DC by 4:30. Have Gordon meet us at the Hay-Adams no later than 5. Also have him keep an eye out for a New York City cab around the hotel. Should be easy to spot. Unless he flew, which I don't see any sign of on his credit cards, he either took a train or a cab to DC."

"Okay, just texted Gordon and he'll circle the area until you arrive just in case McDowell took a cab. Might be better if he doesn't make it to the hotel at all. Call me no later than 5:30."

The two men in suits grabbed some bottled water and Oreos from James' refrigerator then petted his cat on the way out. Within twenty minutes they were searching car to car for James on a high-speed train heading to DC.

CHAPTER 15

"SO IF PEOPLE ALREADY KNOW Obama's going to win, why all this election crap? The conventions, the endless ads on TV, the rallies and all that damn money being spent," David asked.

"It's all part of an election industry," James explained. "Billions of dollars are spent each election cycle, and no one would want that to end. Think of all the jobs that elections create with those consultants and spokespersons you see and hear on the air. The thousands of staff jobs. All the hotel rooms at the conventions. All the food and drinks. The dinners and parties, the donations and fund-raisers. The travel. The hookers. It all adds up to billions of dollars. Besides, only a few people know he's going to win."

"You mean the people fixing the election?"

"No, of course not. Fixing an election at polling places would be far too easy to discover. Such a thing would be almost impossible to pull off. After all, there are thousands of polling locations and tens of thousands of volunteers who would scream bloody murder if they saw something that smelled funny," James said.

"Then who's fixing the election?"

"I never said anyone is directly fixing the election. It's not that people are messing with the ballot boxes, the voting machines, or something like that."

"Then how the hell do you know Obama's going to win today if it's not fixed?"

"It's not fixed the way you think it's fixed."

"Then how is it fixed, or rigged, or already determined, or whatever the hell you want to call it?" David asked, exasperated.

"Very simply there are people who know for certain how voters like you will vote if they get certain statistical input that is repeated time after time over months and even years."

"What does *certain statistical input* mean?"

"It means if you read or hear certain statistical information, certain data, time and time again, you will absorb that information and data over an extended period and accept it as fact. Using a computer comparison, that data enters your intellectual hard drive. It becomes imbedded, and you believe it."

"Makes the voter sound stupid."

"Not stupid, just uninformed. Purposely uninformed. More precisely, misinformed. And in the next election cycle in four years, these disinformation attacks will get worse given the growth of tools like Facebook and Twitter and the involvement of foreign entities," James clarified.

"Reminds me of that movie the *Manchurian Candidate*, you know the one with Frank Sinatra. Good flick."

"Sorta, but that plot was based on a form of hypnotism. What I am talking about is disinformation. You know, fake news."

"Sometimes I think it's all fake. All some kind of show."

"It is in a certain way, but in addition to that information being initially imbedded, you'll continue to roll it around in your head for a few months, have it reinforced by the friends and family in your own private echo chambers, who have heard the same flawed data. You then get even more direct confirmation of the bogus information from dozens of media sources right before the election. Based on all that crap statistical and misinformation input, you'll then vote a certain way based on that erroneous information. It's all really pretty simple stuff. Madison Avenue has been doing it for years. Ever see *Mad Men?*"

"Yeah, great show. But what you just said sounds like bullshit to me. Does Obama know he's going to win?"

"No, of course not." James said as he shook his head at what he perceived as a stupid question.

Not letting a reputation for asking stupid questions deter him, David asked, "Does Romney know he's going to lose?"

"No, David, he doesn't."

"So you're just a pollster."

"A pollster? Haven't you listened to what I'm saying? Pollsters are for the most part, full of shit. They read trends based on the very flawed data I have just described, talk to people, and try to guess what someone will do in a voting booth. Where they really mess up the most is that they also poll many of the 50% of the people in this country who don't ever bother to vote. But those same people tell the pollsters they *will* vote. Ergo, David, the pollsters spit out garbage because they analyze garbage."

"Fifty percent of the people don't vote?"

"That's right. They also don't read or listen or comprehend. Further, they don't care to read, listen, or comprehend. They're called low information non-participants. They might go to a rally, scream and yell at their congressman, but they would rather go to a sale at Walmart on Election Day than go vote. So, we ignore them."

"Who's we?"

"Companies like mine, I mean, the one I used to work for."

"That econo…bullshit."

"The Econometric Forecasting Cooperative."

"Yeah, that thing. I still think you're just guessing."

"Guesswork is taken out of the equation as soon as people like you begin believing the numbers and the bullshit information you hear. You believe it because you want to believe it. And we will crank out those numbers and that info until you do believe it all. We spend billions each election to insure you will believe all that stuff. And you do. It's all numbers, all statistics. All mean, median, mode. Hell, it's really just all fourth grade arithmetic."

"What if people like me didn't believe the numbers and voted for Romney anyway?"

"As a group, you won't. First of all, people don't usually like change. Give them half a chance, and they'll keep the status quo. But if they demand change, like back in 1980 with Reagan replacing Carter, I learned just recently that we make sure they hear the numbers and statistics we want them to hear, so the change they get is the change we want them to have. Besides, now it's the Democrats' turn."

"Turn?"

"Look back over the last sixty years. With the exception of Bush One following Reagan, which was agreed on, administrations have alternated power since Truman. That's the deal."

"What deal?"

"Power is money. Administrations need time to make money unless those making the decisions see another way to make cash like with Bush One and the Persian Gulf War. You really think Dukakis would have invaded Iraq? Hell no. So the twelve years of Reagan and Bush was agreed on by our groups, including Clinton being put in place in 1992, although he almost blew it with all the women. Forgive the pun."

"So all the candidates go through this charade already knowing if they are going to win or lose?"

"Christ, of course not. Their parties don't even know. You could never keep that kind of thing quiet that far down the food chain."

"Sorry. I still think you're kind of full of shit. I mean, you're a nice guy and all, but full of shit. Besides, why would you tell me this stuff if it was true?"

"Look, like I said, I just recently learned how all this works by reading years of files and memos, so I don't have all the answers yet, but I know people who do, and I'm going to make sure all the right questions are asked. Besides, it's not like you have your own talk show now, is it?"

"Not yet," David admitted.

"Over the last month I've been doing research and compiling data, very accurate data that I'm going to share with the world. In fact, I'm going to DC to tape a show for C-Span tomorrow morning for airing on Sunday."

"What are you going to say?"

"I'm going to tell the world the whole story, everything I'm telling you now. How the winners of every presidential election since 1952 have been preselected and put in power by a small group of men and women who make billions each year by controlling that process. It's all going to come out in the open…finally."

"Damn, so you're saying all these rich Super PAC guys have been rigging our elections for sixty years. Man, what a story."

"David, it's not the rich PAC guys; it's not the parties or the candidates. It's the guys who come up with the numbers. The stats guys. Guys like me. We rule the world."

David shook his head in disbelief. He then glanced in his rearview mirror and saw the distinctive grille of a black Audi S-8 and its arching front lights. He said nothing to James. Instead he looked up and saw a sign: *I-395 Ahead. Washington DC, 1 Mile.*

"We're almost there, James. Where on Pennsylvania Avenue?"

"In front of the FBI Building."

"You got it."

Minutes later, as David's cab crawled through rush-hour traffic, he saw the Audi again in his rearview mirror while he waited at a stoplight. The driver was on his cell.

CHAPTER 16

"I PICKED UP A NEW York City cab a few minutes ago. I think it's him. Passed them once and it looks like him in the back seat. There can't be too many New York cabs down here. I'm right behind them now." Gordon said.

From her New York office, Connie made a corporate decision. "He needs to be contained."

"Yes, ma'am. That's a roger."

"It would be particularly beneficial if he were not to make it to his hotel."

"That might be a little difficult with all the traffic and people walkin' around. ma'am."

"If it were easy, Gordon, you would not be on my payroll."

"Yes ma'am."

CHAPTER 17

DAVID SAW THE DRIVER OF the Audi talking on his cell. "That's funny, we've had this Audi on our butts for several minutes now."

On hearing David's news, James turned to look, while at the same time sliding down in his seat. "Oh God, I knew they'd follow me. I have to get out of here!" In seconds James had gathered up his two briefcases and lunged for the street side back passenger door handle while the cab was still moving.

"Hey, what the hell are you doing, James? You want to get yourself killed!?" David yelled.

He slammed on the brakes, and the cab screeched to a stop. When the back door flew open, James stumbled from the cab just as the Audi cut from behind and plowed into the cab's open back door. The door was ripped off its hinges and sent through the air in tandem with James. While the cab's door landed on G Street, James landed on the hood of David's cab. He slid onto the pavement and flipped over several times finally landing on his right shoulder and hip. In his hand was one of the large briefcases he had had in the cab.

David yelled out the window to his fallen passenger. "James, are you alright!? You want me to take you to the hospital?" When James rose, he looked at David with his eyes opened wide in fear. He turned and limped away through a growing crowd that had gathered in seconds to see what they could see.

The driver of the Audi, not wishing to create any more traffic issues, sped away and tried to disappear into rush hour traffic. At seeing his disconnected door, and the fleeing Audi, all David could say to himself was, "Damn, me and my $2,000 deductible."

After he left the cab and quickly retrieved his door from the street, David tossed it in the back seat, jumped back into the driver's seat and made a spur-of-the-moment personal decision. The decision was that he definitely didn't want to get involved with DC police while he was driving a New York City cab especially after someone in a big ass Audi had nailed his passenger. So he too left the scene and halfheartedly tried to chase down the Audi but gave up after a few blocks.

On his way back to I-95 North, David mentally relived his bizarre yet profitable day. But the most amazing aspect of the day was the fact James could actually walk away from what had just happened to him.

He also wondered how much his insurance was going to go up because some asshole from DC just lopped off his door.

CHAPTER 18

Hay-Adams Hotel, Washington, DC

STRIPPED DOWN TO HIS PLAID boxer shorts and black socks, James laid on his king-size bed in the Hay-Adams Hotel in some serious pain while he flipped between C-Span, CNN, and Fox News. He liked to keep informed even as his shoulder throbbed.

He also wanted to get the hang of how guests were interviewed so when he became a media star for uncovering how the country had been deprived of its collective vote, even though the Constitution does not guarantee it, he would be ready to respond to all those media types. His thoughts of becoming rich and famous made him think of Marsha and his unfulfilled plan.

As he flipped the buttons on the remote control, he grimaced but had decided not to take any of the pain medication he had seen in the hotel gift shop. He feared the meds could dull his senses when he made his network television debut, even though it was only C-Span. *I have to start somewhere*, he thought to himself.

He suspected he had suffered a broken collarbone from his run-in with the Audi, along with a severely bruised hip, a sprained ankle, and assorted cuts, scrapes and bruises. He had called the producer he was talking to from C-Span and told her about his accident, but she was less than sympathetic. "Why can't you come here and do one of those mobile interviews I see all the time on TV?" James had asked.

When told it would be too expensive and if he wanted to tell his story he would have to make his way to the station, James was not amused. "I may have a broken collar bone and sprained ankle, and I think I was hit by a car on purpose because of what I'll be telling you guys tomorrow."

Not budging, the producer told James he would have to be at the station no later than nine a.m. the next morning, or the interview would have to be rescheduled. The fact was, the producer thought James was full of shit. The second such opinion James had received that day.

James finally admitted defeat and said, "Okay, I'll be there by 9."

He did not bother to tell the producer that all the statistical proof of his story in the briefcase was no longer in his possession. It had either dropped onto G Street after he was hit, or it was still in the back of David's cab. James tried to remember the name of the cab company but could not.

His only hope was that the briefcase was still in the cab, and David, being a seemingly honest sort, would find his contact info and let him know he had in his possession what James had lost. If in fact the briefcase had landed in the street however, James knew it was probably lost forever.

While the lost briefcase was a temporary inconvenience given his later appearance on C-Span, he knew he could always make fresh copies from the flash drive he had hidden in his apartment in a bag of kitty litter.

He was working on his presentation notes on a yellow tablet when there was a knock on his door. "Who is it?"

"Dr. McDowell, we are from C-Span and wanted to discuss some items before tomorrow's taping."

"Oh, really? Okay great…just a minute."

James got out of bed, limped to the closet, found the thick white terrycloth robe he had seen earlier, and slipped it on. He checked his hair in the mirror, decided it was hopeless, and moved to the door.

When he opened the door, he was greeted by two well-dressed smiling men in expensive suits who carried expensive briefcases. "Good evening, Dr. McDowell. I am John Mercer, and this is my co-producer, Mr. Richard Reyes, and we are here to go over some of the questions you will be asked tomorrow and get a basic understanding of what you will be presenting."

After shaking the men's hands James said, "Come on in. Boy, you guys sure have lots of producers. I just talked to Miss Davis a while ago and she said…"

"Miss Davis is just an associate producer, strictly administrative work, you know, really just a secretary. We are the actual producers of the show. She works for us."

"Well, this TV stuff is new to me so… whatever."

"This won't take long, Dr. McDowell. All we need is an idea of what you'll be presenting tomorrow so we can prepare the necessary graphics and charts to assist the audience in understanding what you are saying."

"That's cool."

After asking and getting some basic information from James, Mr. Mercer, a tan, slender, darkly handsome man with salt and pepper hair who could have easily passed as a maître d' at a fancy DC restaurant asked, "So doctor, what will be your basic thesis during tomorrow's interview?"

"First of all, this is not a thesis or some kind of crazy UFO theory. I have hard, concrete, empirical proof, that a group of very wealthy individuals in this country has, since 1952, selected every one of our presidents by producing fake data and information that is disseminated through all media platforms to ensure the outcome of an election. Further, that this same group will hand-select the president they want and then ensure his or her election by flooding the media with false information."

"That is quite an assertion, Dr. McDowell." Richard Reyes said with just the slightest Hispanic accent. Even sitting, it was clear Mr. Reyes was a large man. Not fat, just big. Not real tall, just thick, very thick. He had short cropped hair and appeared to be in his early forties.

"I know, but like I said, I have proof. I have all the stats to back me up and once I can show what I have, I think this could be a *New York Times* front page story." James said proudly.

"I don't doubt that for a moment, Doctor, but you said you have documented proof. What kind of proof, and do you have that proof with you?"

"To tell you the truth, I had all the proof with me earlier today but…well, you may not believe this, but I was hit by a car this afternoon right in front of the FBI Building on Pennsylvania Avenue and lost one of my two briefcases with all my stuff, you know, my proof, in it. Not sure where it is now."

"So, you are saying you no longer have your proof?" Mr. Mercer asked with a smile.

"I have it, I have it all, but just not with me."

"So you lost one of your briefcases, the one with all your proof, is that right?"

"Yes, like I said I was hit by this big car, and one of my briefcases was just gone."

"Well, I am afraid to say this creates a problem for us at C-Span. Unless you have some kind of documentation to back up your claims, we can't let you go on the air under our banner of objectivity and risk our reputation by simply espousing some far-out conspiracy theory."

"It's not a conspiracy theory! I have the proof, just not with me."

"Then where is it that proof, Doctor?" Mr. Mercer asked with smile.

"It's…well…it's" James was beginning to feel uncomfortable with all the questions and even more uncomfortable when he saw Mr. Reyes rise from his chair and move toward him. "All my backup data is back in New York."

"Where in New York, Doctor?" the still-smiling Mr. Mercer asked.

After a few moments, James said, "I think I've changed my mind. I don't want to go on C-Span…"

"Where the fuck is the information, asshole?" a non-smiling Mr. Reyes asked.

"Hey, who are you guys?" James asked, afraid of the answer.

Moving far quicker than one might suspect given his thickness, the three-hundred pound Mr. Reyes lunged at James with a white cloth in his hand that he jammed against James' mouth and nose. After a futile effort to defend himself against the now smiling Mr. Reyes, James passed out from the ether he had inhaled.

CHAPTER 19

ON THE NOISY DRIVE BACK to New York from DC, thanks to the unattached rear passenger door, David called Syd and told her what had happened with this weird fare he had picked up and driven to Pennsylvania Avenue. He also told her that they were now independently wealthy, at least for the night, given the ten one hundred dollar bills he had in his shirt pocket. After a few graphic promises from David that led Syd to believe that sexual nirvana was in her immediate future, they said good-bye.

Yet, as the miles rolled past, David couldn't forget everything James had told him. If what he said was true, and David had serious doubts that any of it was true, the very foundation of the country was, according to James, an utter and complete sham. The idea that a handful of companies could control the electorate in such a way seemed preposterous to David.

At the same time, James didn't talk like a crazy guy. He was clearly intelligent, educated, and obviously upset that the information he had uncovered was important enough that a driver in a black Audi tried to kill him only a few blocks from the White House.

David marveled that James was able to get up from the pavement after being nailed by the Audi and walk away from the scene of the accident, albeit with a decided limp. James was tougher than he looked, David concluded. But James also seemed genuinely afraid that people were after him for what he knew. Maybe even for what he had in those two briefcases.

As Manhattan loomed in the distance, David wondered what would happen if James actually got on C-Span and told his story. He told himself he would look at his cable TV schedule and check it out. He realized it would be the first time he ever watched C-Span.

CHAPTER 20

JAMES LAY NAKED AND UNCONSCIOUS on a king-size bed in the sumptuous bedroom with the door closed, a washcloth stuff in his mouth. Mercer and "Big Rico" Reyes raided the suite's refrigerator looking for goodies. They found a treasure trove of assorted drinks, peanuts, candy bars, crackers, cheese, and even some beef jerky. They began to feast.

After several minutes, they were interrupted by a knock on the door. They didn't answer. "Room service, sir, sorry it took so long."

"About time, come on in." Mercer said with a shrug as he smiled at Big Rico.

"Sorry sir, we're not allowed to enter a room without..."

"Damn, okay, give me a minute."

With his ever-present smile on his face, Mercer opened the door slightly, peeked out, and said to the young waiter, "I just got out of the shower, please just push the cart in, and I'll sign the check. Bet you'd like a nice tip, wouldn't you?"

"Yes sir, whatever you think is fair."

"I think a $100 tip is fair, don't you, young man?"

"Oh, yes sir! And when you're through, just dial 8 and I'll come get your tray."

After he signed the check with the promised tip attached, Mercer pulled in the food cart and lifted the metal plate covers and saw a thick steak, fries, a tossed salad, and chocolate cream pie. At the same time, a muffled sound emanated from the bedroom. James was awake, and he didn't sound happy.

CHAPTER 21

JAMES TRIED TO OPEN HIS eyes and focus on his surroundings. Where was he? What day was it? What time was it? What was he doing in a damn bed? So many questions and no answers.

He tried to move but couldn't. Was he paralyzed? No, it was the zip ties. There were nylon fasteners secured tightly around his wrists and ankles, which had been anchored to the bed frame. His naked spread-eagled body was propped up against the headboard by several 800-count Egyptian cotton pillows, giving him a clear view of the bedroom and the door to the adjacent living room.

How did this happen? It was those two men—the men from C-Span. They weren't from C-Span. C-Span wouldn't tie him up. At least he didn't think they would.

Mercer entered the room and smiled at James. "Have a nice rest, doctor?" Big Rico entered right behind Mercer, carrying his expensive briefcase. He wasn't smiling.

James tried to talk, but his brain was still a bit sluggish and the wash cloth was still stuck in his mouth.

"I was hoping your rest might have a positive impact on your memory," Mercer added.

James said something back that could have been "Untie me you fucking assholes." But it came out as a muted "umptymiufkgassoes."

Moving to James' bedside, Mercer said, "Doctor, I'd prefer to call you James, if you don't mind, and feel free to call me John. I really like to keep these kinds of things on an informal basis. In a few minutes, I'm going to come back in this room and ask you some questions. If you answer them fully and truthfully, then we will be on our way and things will be fine. If not, then I'm afraid my friend here—you can call him Big Rico if you like—has ways of improving your memory. While he prepares to do that, I am going to go back in the other room, finish *your* steak dinner, and watch ESPN."

James tried to say something else, but it came out all wrong, so he just made a sound that was between an extended moan and a grunt.

After Mercer left the bedroom, Big Rico stared at James for several moments then took off his suit coat, tie, shirt, and pants. He folded them neatly over a dressing room chair. All that remained were Speedo looking black undershorts, black shoes, and black socks that were held up with stylish black elastic garters.

Absent his $1500 suit, $300 shirt and $200 tie, Big Rico looked a bit like a sumo wrestler, except he wasn't Asian, didn't have a chonmage, and wasn't hairless. In fact, he had a significant amount of hair all over his body, especially on his back, which appeared long enough that it could have been braided. He smelled like a combination of cheap aftershave and sweat.

From an ankle holster, he pulled out a large serrated edged knife and lay it within James' line of sight on the bedside table. From his back pants pockets, he retrieved two white surgical gloves and slipped them on his thick albeit dexterous hands and fingers.

From his briefcase he pulled out a large white tube and placed it on the bed next to James' pillow. He also removed a flat leather box, opened it carefully, and placed it next to the tube. That elicited from James another unintelligible sound when he saw that the box contained over a dozen glistening scalpels, surgical knives, and small saw capable of cutting through flesh and bone. The tools were laid out in the box on thick green felt.

Saying nothing, Big Rico picked up the tube, squirted a handful of a clear jelly like substance into his hand and began to rub it over James' body. James' eyes were wide open in fear, but he had given up trying to scream. The gel was cold. It smelled fresh, like leaves or grass or something James couldn't put his finger on.

After applying the gel to every part of James' body, Big Rico sat in a chair, picked up a travel magazine from an end table, and read an article about the fine foods of Italy.

CHAPTER 22

IN THE LIVING ROOM OF James' suite, Mercer watched a rerun of the 1964 Browns–Colts championship game on ESPN3, while he leisurely ate a tender Delmonico steak, surprisingly good steak fries, and a crisp tossed salad. He topped it off with a smooth and very satisfying piece of chocolate cream pie. The small bottle of merlot he had selected from the hotel refrigerator was below average.

He was tempted to sit a few more minutes, relax, and watch a replay of the 1975 World Series that was coming on next, but he always hated how that series ended. Instead, he decided it was time to get back to work.

When he entered James' bedroom, Mercer flipped on the radio and searched until he found a soft rock station that happened to be playing a tribute to the Eagles, his favorite band. He carefully adjusted the volume to the point where James' voice wouldn't be heard but not so loud that someone would complain to the hotel manager over "Tequila Sunrise."

Mercer noticed that Big Rico was relaxed in a chair as he read a magazine, while James appeared a bit tense as he lay naked on the bed, his eyes large as saucers. The strange sounds coming from his cloth-filled mouth had evolved into a kind of a whimper. James' body was lathered in a clear gel from head to toe, and it glistened in the muted half-light of a bedroom lamp.

"James, I must say your selection for dinner was excellent. I think you would've really enjoyed that pie. Just like mom used to make."

James made another strange sound that Mercer ignored.

"As I mentioned a few minutes ago, I am now going to ask you some questions. If I think you have answered my questions honestly, then Big Rico here will stay just where he is on that chair. Of course, if I think you are being dishonest in your answers, then…well let's just say you may not enjoy what Big Rico does to you. Do you understand what I am saying, James?"

With eyes now the size of dinner plates, James nodded emphatically as "Hotel California" played in the background.

"Good, glad we understand each other. By the way, we don't wish to cause you unnecessary discomfort so Big Rico here has been considerate and covered you with a potent gel form of lidocaine that will deaden most pain for up to two hours. After all, pain causes discomfort and also generates aggravating noises that we find distasteful and annoying. We hope you appreciate Big Rico's efforts on your behalf."

Big Rico smiled at James. The sounds coming from James were

now at a higher pitch, and he kept shaking his head from side to side.

"Okay James, now I am going to ask Big Rico to remove your gag, but if you cry out, he will use that very large knife to silence you. Understand?" James nodded as Big Rico sat on the bed and pulled the washcloth from James' mouth. "Now James, tell me where the second briefcase is." Mercer asked softly.

James tried to talk, but his throat was dry and raw and he had trouble forming words. "I... I ... had two briefcases... then I was hit by that car... and there was only one. Maybe it fell on the street or maybe it's in the cab...dear God, I don't know where it is...I would tell you. I swear."

"James I must say, I just don't believe you. Do you believe James, Big Rico?"

"No, boss. I think he's lying to us."

"I do too." Mercer nodded to Big Rico who took a thin scalpel from the green felt and without hesitation ran its blade twelve inches down James' right leg from his upper thigh to the top of his knee. The razor-sharp steel going through James' flesh made no sound, and at first it was if nothing had happened. There was no pain, no screaming, not even any blood—only an almost imperceptible line on his leg left by the gleaming surgical tool.

Although shocked at what he was seeing happen to his leg, the lack of pain made it all the more surreal to James, like it was happening to someone else. But then blood slowly appeared along the line and began to seep in red rivulets down his leg onto the bed.

Even without the associated pain, the blood created an urgency in James. He pulled on the plastic ties already knowing they wouldn't release their grip. He pleaded, "No, please don't do this." I'm telling you the truth, I swear."

"Let me ask you again, where is the briefcase, James?"

"Oh, God, I am telling you the truth, I would give you whatever you want, but I don't have it. Someone may have picked it up off the street, or like I said maybe it's still in that cab."

"What was the name of the cab company?"

"I don't remember...it was yellow with red trim...I think."

"You think it was yellow with red trim and you don't remember the name? James, I don't think you are being honest with us again." Mercer said as he once again nodded to Big Rico.

This time the big man made two cuts on James' thigh at either end of the fresh wound he had just made, fashioning a quasi-capital "I". He took out a delicate pair of forceps and used them to peel back the skin on either side of the vertical line of the "I."

Still, there was no pain, yet what he was seeing being done to him made James drift from consciousness to another place in his mind. A safer place. But then he would, despite himself, return to his appalling reality.

He saw Rico take out a thicker scalpel and use it to open up a longer, deeper slash in his left leg, this time starting at his knee and moving upward toward his crotch. The blade stopped near the crease that separated the upper thigh from the torso. This time the blood was instantaneous, and the skin separated until several layers of skin, fat and muscle tissue could be seen, no flaying necessary.

"James, where is the briefcase?" he thought he heard someone say but wasn't quite sure.

While he still felt no pain, James' face became white as he gaped at the mutilation of his legs, and he felt a wave of nausea overcome him. "I'm going to be sick," James whispered. He then turned his head toward Big Rico and vomited, covering Rico in fetid chunks.

"You fucking asshole, these are brand new shoes." Big Rico said as he backhanded James with the thick scalpel that left a deep slice in his right cheek that penetrated all the way to his tongue. Blood poured from James' mouth and trickled down his bare chest onto the sheets beneath him that had already turned a deep crimson from the leg wounds.

Trying once more to elicit the information he had been sent to collect, Mercer said in a calm, low voice, "James, if you don't know where the briefcase is, where is the information you said you have in New York?"

"My apartment…it's in my apartment," James mumbled.

"No, it's not, James. We've already looked there, you're lying again." Mercer said.

"Kitty litter…" James slurred.

"I must say, James, I am beginning to believe you. But if you really don't know where the briefcase is, you are of no further use to us."

James heard Mercer's voice but couldn't understand a word he was saying. He was in that safe place again. No pain and quiet.

"But there are people who insist you stole from them. They feel you are a definite threat to them and need to be punished, James."

James felt something that forced him to return from the safe place. It was his leg, then both legs. Then there was something else. He thought of Marsha.

"And James, I may have told you a little white lie about the gel Big Rico put on you. It only lasts about fifteen minutes."

Fuck him, James thought. He also thought of Rocky.

As James watched, Big Rico took a larger, thicker scalpel and slashed James from throat to crotch in a single motion. For several seconds, James didn't feel any pain. But slowly a burning sensation began in his abdomen and spread in both directions. It felt like he was being burned by a blow torch.

He wanted to go back to the safe, quiet space. He could hear "There's Gonna Be a Heartache Tonight" in the background. He would drift off, then awake in agony and see Big Rico's angry face. He could see him slashing and slashing with the scalpel but fuck him too. James decided it was time to go to that safe place and never come back.

CHAPTER 23

AFTER THE LONG, LOUD DRIVE back from DC, David pulled into the garage and turned off the lights. In a few minutes Gino, the owner of the small cab company, entered the garage. He was a large, nearly bald man in his seventies, originally from a small town in Tuscany. "What the fuck?"

"I had this fare who took a dive on me."

"Is the stupid bastard dead?"

"No, but I think he could be hurt pretty bad. He bailed street side and got clipped by a big ass Audi that drove off after knocking him up on the hood. Think my fare thought the guy who hit him was chasing him."

"Looks like he caught him to me. Well, that'll be a damn lawsuit. Are you okay?"

"I'm fine. I tried to get my guy to stop after he got hit, but he wouldn't. It was a hit and run all the way and not a cop in sight. Right in front of the damn FBI Building too."

"Never one around when you need one."

"I'm sorry, Gino, I tried to tell the guy not to get out street side but he…"

"Shit happens…cost of doing business. Fuck it, that's why I got insurance. I'll get Eddie to throw on the door in the morning. You should be good to go tomorrow afternoon."

"Thanks, Gino. You know I have my own insurance and…"

"I'll take care of it. You just keep writing and don't worry about this kind of shit."

"Thanks, Gino, I really appreciate it. I'll clean her out and gas up now so she's ready first thing. See you tomorrow and thanks again."

Gino turned, waved his hand in the air, and started to enter his small row home next to the garage. "Hey, you and that pretty wife of yours still coming over for spaghetti tomorrow night?"

"Of course, we wouldn't miss it. Tell Marie we'll bring the wine."

"Sure. You know, Marie thinks Sydney looks like that old actress Natalie Wood. I always liked Natalie Wood. She was really great in *Splendor in the Grass*. Too bad she couldn't swim. See you guys tomorrow night." Gino waved again and left the garage.

After Gino was gone, David reached into his shirt pocket and pulled out the ten one hundred dollar bills James had given him. When he had called Syd earlier and told her about the strange guy who had given him the cash and then got hit by a car, she told him to hurry home so they could still watch *The Big Chill* on AMC. He told her he would and that he was now willing and able to pay for sexual favors. For several minutes they negotiated price and terms.

David took the portable vacuum and began to clean out the cab. When he got to the back seat he found James' second briefcase wedged firmly under the front passenger seat. Attached to the briefcase was an ID tag with James' name, address, and cell phone number on it. Sticking out of one pocket of the briefcase was the confirmation for a room at the Hay-Adams in DC. James' cell phone was in the other pocket.

After he removed the briefcase, David couldn't help but look inside. He was disappointed that all he found were hundreds of papers in a half-dozen file folders. When he opened some of the files, the endless numbers and statistics gave him a headache, and he remembered how he hated the Statistics 101 class he was forced to take back at NYU.

He returned the papers to the briefcase, finished cleaning the cab, grabbed his license from the dashboard holder, and walked back to his apartment. On the way, he remembered one of the things Syd said she would do for the right amount of cold hard cash. The thought of such an act made him walk faster and with more purpose.

David entered his apartment and placed the briefcase on the kitchen table. "Hey Luuucy, I'm hoooome." He announced in his best Desi Arnaz impression, which by his own admission was not very good.

From the bedroom Syd had a suggestion, "Let's go out for dinner tonight. It's too late to cook."

"We can't, we're broke."

"What about the grand you made today. You said we were rich on the phone."

"I already spent it on roadside sex and porno DVDs but don't worry, they're in HD." David said as he looked through a stack of mail, noticing mostly bills.

"That's okay, I made some extra money today turning tricks at the bus station after work."

"That's my girl. Only hope it wasn't all quarters again, like last time."

"Quarters are all those eighth grade boys have."

Syd entered the living room wearing a tight red sweater and equally tight black jeans.

"Damn, if you wore that outfit down to the bus station, I'd bet you make at least ten bucks."

"Smartass."

"Come here, woman." David pulled Syd close and kissed her while he grabbed her butt. She kissed him back and grabbed his. After some additional groping, Syd saw the briefcase on the table.

"Where did you get that?"

"The guy who got hit by the car must have dropped it in the back seat when he got nailed. I just found it a few minutes ago when I was cleaning out the cab at Gino's. I better give the guy a call and let him know I got it."

"Call him on the way, I'm hungry. Mexican?"

CHAPTER 24

AFTER LEAVING JAMES AT THE Hay-Adams, Mercer and Big Rico were picked up by Gordon in the Audi S-8 and made it back to Manhattan in record time where their day had started. They went directly to James' apartment building to visit a cat.

Gordon waited in the Audi while Mercer and Big Rico got inside the building as they had done earlier in the day. They were stunned when they opened the apartment door.

The place they had left in shambles only hours before was now neat and clean. It had been picked up, vacuumed, the trash emptied, and bathroom cleaned by someone who had even folded up the end of the toilet paper roll like the hotels do to let you know someone had been there. The apartment also smelled like Pine Sol and furniture wax.

"He mentioned the kitty litter." Mercer said.

"Here kitty, kitty, kitty." Big Rico said in a high pitched voice.

"Do you think the damn cat is going to tell you where his litter is?" Mercer asked while he shook his head.

"Well..."

"Look around for the litter box or a bag of litter in the kitchen, I'll check the other rooms."

After a short recon mission, no litter bag or litter box was discovered. In fact, there was no cat to be found. However, Mercer did find a note on the kitchen cabinet. *"Mr. James. You did not tell me the place was so messy. Was very surprised, not like you. I took Rocky and his food, his treats, litter box, and litter like you asked me to. Call me when you come back."* R.

"Shit, somebody picked up that litter. Let's get over to the garage and see if we can find out anything from the guy who owns the cab."

"Yes sir, boss." Big Rico said with anticipation.

CHAPTER 25

AFTER A MAID HAD DISCOVERED James' body during a turn-down service, she alerted the hotel guests and management of what had happened by running and screaming down the hall. Less than an hour later, veteran Detective Robert Casey entered the suite.

Several DC cops and EMTs were already sitting around the room and telling the oft repeated dead-guy jokes that Casey had heard a hundred times before over a twenty-five-year career. When the cops saw Casey enter, they suddenly shut up and rose as the "Boss," as Casey was known, looked over the scene. In the bedroom formerly occupied by James, Casey saw the outline of a body on the floor covered by a white blood stained sheet.

When he nodded to have the sheet pulled back, he saw that James had been sliced and diced by someone who knew what they were doing. By someone who liked what they were doing. The odd thing about the eviscerated body that Casey was looking at was the face appeared remarkably calm. There was no trace of fear, agony, or suffering. "Was he alive during all this?" Casey asked the coroner.

"Looks like it."

"What's that smell?"

"Lidocaine. It's all over his body. That's why there's no sign of a struggle. There was also ether used to knock him out probably before the cutting started."

"You think he was awake during all this? I mean, did he see himself being cut up?"

"Looks like it."

As he stared at the mutilated body, Casey asked, "Wonder who he pissed off?"

"Not sure, Detective, but I'd guess it was somebody who has done this before."

"What kind of tools did they use?"

"Given the kinds of cuts and incisions, it looks like surgical grade stuff."

"Is that what I think it is in his mouth?"

"Yeah."

"That was kind of rude. Hope the poor bastard was already dead when they did that."

After Casey left the bedroom he moved slowly around the rest of the suite, while two photographers from the coroner's office began snapping pictures of the crime scene.

"Looks like someone had dinner." Casey said to no one in particular.

CHAPTER 26

DAVID AND SYD WALKED DOWN the street in the West Village hand-in-hand toward El Toro's, their favorite Mexican joint. On the way, David called the Hay-Adams using James' phone. "Dr. James McDowell's room please."

"One moment, sir," the switchboard operator said to David. She turned to her manager and said, "It's a call for the guy in 633."

"The cop said to let any calls through," the manager responded with a shrug.

CHAPTER 27

AS CASEY MOVED TO LOOK in the bathroom of the suite, the phone rang. He motioned for the others in the room to shut up. He answered the phone on speaker.

"Hello."

"Hey, James, this is David, your cabbie from this afternoon."

"Oh, yeah."

"You okay, man? I thought that Audi got you pretty good."

"I'm okay."

"I saw where you were staying and just called to let you know you left your briefcase in the back of my cab. Didn't find it until I got back to New York tonight."

"That's great. Where is the briefcase now?"

David stopped walking and asked, "James, your voice sounds funny. You okay, man?"

"Where's the briefcase now, David? I'll have someone pick it up tomorrow morning." Casey said.

"Is this James? This doesn't sound like..."

Casey suddenly dropped the ruse. "David, my name is Detective Robert Casey of

the Washington DC Violent Crimes Unit. Am I to understand you drove Dr. McDowell from New York to his hotel earlier today?"

"Wait a minute, who did you say you were?"

"My name is Detective Casey, DC Police."

"Did something happen to James?"

"David, please answer my question, did you drive Dr. McDowell from New York to DC?"

"Tell me what the hell happened to James."

"He was murdered in his room tonight."

"What!?"

"David, what time did you deliver him to the hotel?"

"I didn't. He jumped out of my cab near Pennsylvania and G Street and got hit by this big black Audi. But he got up by himself and disappeared into the crowd. I didn't know where he was staying until I got back here and saw his hotel confirmation in his briefcase."

"Why did he jump from your cab?"

"Don't really know except for the fact he got big time freaked out when I said I thought that Audi was following us."

"What time were you in DC?"

"Around 4:30."

"David, what is your last name and what cab company do you work for?"

"Why do you want to know that?"

"I'd like to send one of our detectives to New York and take your statement and pick up the briefcase and speak with you."

"About what?"

"First of all, you left the scene of an accident and…"

The phone in the suite went dead. Casey quickly called the front desk. "This is Detective Casey. Was there a caller ID on the call that just came into this room?"

"Yes, sir. It said the call was from a James McDowell," the front desk operator reported.

CHAPTER 28

DAVID CLICKED OFF JAMES' PHONE and stood in stunned silence under a streetlamp. "What's wrong, honey?" Syd asked.

"That guy I took to DC this afternoon, James—he was murdered in his room tonight."

"Oh my God, David."

"I can't believe that guy's dead."

"Who were you talking to?"

"Some homicide detective, I guess. He asked me a bunch of questions. He wants to send a detective up here to question me."

"Does he think you killed the guy?"

David looked at Syd like she was nuts. "Are you nuts? If I'd killed the guy, why would I call his hotel? To tell him I'm sorry? I mean, I don't think he thinks I killed the guy. Do you think he thinks I killed the guy?"

"Maybe you better call him back and tell him what you know."

"I told him everything I know already. I sure as hell don't want to get involved in some murder investigation. Having Yellow Cab on my resume's bad enough."

"Can they trace your call, like in the movies?"

"Well, they can do something called cellular triangulation, but it won't do them much good since this isn't my phone."

"What about those cell phone 'pings' I've heard about?"

"That's easy," David said. After he wiped off his fingerprints from the phone, David looked around, saw no one, and tossed James' phone into a water-filled sewer.

Later at El Toro, David and Syd had beers after dinner. "Did you look in that guy's briefcase?" Syd asked.

"Yeah, but all I saw was a lot of papers with a bunch of numbers and statistics. He had told me he was a 'stats guy.' Guess he was."

"Anything that looked like it would make somebody want to run over him?"

"Nothing I could see. Like I said, it was just a bunch of files and papers."

"When we get back, I'll take a look and see if I can understand any of it. We should also check the net and see if there's a story posted yet." Syd said.

"Good idea. He sure seemed nervous. Said he was going to go on TV Sunday and spill his guts over some information he'd discovered."

"Do you think someone could be murdered over numbers?" Syd

asked.

"Guess that depends on what the numbers are. But he was sure uptight over the idea of somebody following him."

"David, if the guy in the Audi killed James, do you think they saw you and the cab?"

"I don't know. I guess a New York City cab would stand out in DC."

"How tough would it be to track down your cab's number?"

"Each cab's number is on the side of the cab. That medallion number is registered on the internet next to the cab's ID Number and the owner's address."

David and Syd sat in silence for several moments. "I know it's after midnight, but maybe we should call Gino," Syd said.

David nodded and dialed Gino and Marie's number on Syd's phone. After several rings, David said, "No answer."

"Maybe they're asleep, and Gino turned off his cell."

"I dialed their home number."

"Let's walk over."

"What if we wake them?"

"So what? This is important."

CHAPTER 29

BEFORE TRYING THE HOUSE, DAVID and Syd first entered Gino's garage with David's key. He tried the overhead light, but it didn't work. "Did it work earlier tonight?" Syd asked.

"Yeah, it worked fine."

Light from the overhead streetlamps filtered into the garage, and David could see his cab in the grayness. The cab looked the same as it did earlier in the evening, except for one thing. "I shut this back door before I left."

"You sure?"

"Positive."

"Maybe Gino came out and..."

A barking dog interrupted Syd and David's conversation. David walked toward the connecting door to Gino's row house from the garage. He tried the door. It opened. "Gino always kept this door locked," David whispered. "You stay here; I'm going in to check things out."

"Like hell you are." Syd whispered back and moved through the doorway with David.

As soon as they entered the row house, they could see lights on in the kitchen. "Hey Gino, it's David and Syd. Just wanted to make sure you guys are alright. Hey Gino, you there?"

"Marie, it's me, Sydney, you guys okay?"

David moved into the darkened living room and tried to find the light switch on the wall. Finally, he did, and the room was awash in light. At first, David couldn't comprehend what he was seeing. Only when Syd said, "Oh, my dear God," did his brain kick into gear, and he saw Gino in his favorite La-Z-Boy recliner.

Gino's throat had been cut ear-to-ear, the wound so deep his spinal cord was visible. Blood had saturated his white T-shirt and formed a red pool between his legs on the chair that in turn created a larger pool of blood on the floor. In the corner of the room, Marie was on her back on the floor with a dozen stab wounds in her chest. Their living room had been torn apart by someone looking for something.

"We need to go," David said.

Syd moved to Gino's side and stared into his lifeless eyes.

"Syd, we have to go...now."

"The police, we have to call the police," Syd's voice was a monotone.

"We will, but let's get out of here now."

David took Syd's arm and moved her toward the garage they had come from only moments before. As soon as they entered the garage and approached the large door leading to the street, it was pushed shut from the outside. The garage was thrown into utter blackness.

"Someone's out there," Syd whispered.

"Shhh, come over here."

Using memory instead of sight, David led Syd to the far corner of the garage behind a second cab. He gently pulled her down on the floor. On the way, he had reached out to a nearby workbench, felt around a few seconds, and grabbed a claw hammer.

The silence and darkness in the garage seemed to emphasize the cacophony of odors that were suddenly all around Syd and David. For some reason the darkness heightened the sense of smell. David could smell the oil on the floor, gasoline, rubber, road dirt, and sweaty passengers.

Gino always tried to hide the odors in the interiors of the cabs with a bunch of cheap deodorizers he would buy at flea markets then hang from the rearview mirrors of the cars to make them smell better. They didn't smell better.

David and Syd sat side by side on the floor of the garage in the darkness and the smells and waited for another sound. As usual, Syd was able to fall asleep no matter what the circumstances. She claimed it was because she didn't have a guilty conscience. Conversely, she explained to David that if he confessed all his sins to her, he would be able to fall asleep as easily as she did. David's response was he'd rather not sleep.

As Syd slept, David thought of other nights when he would not sleep, especially those hellish nights during Hell Week. Had he known there were going to be even worse nights in his life than those, he may have quit his quest to become a SEAL. Because the nights did get worse.

There were nights when he and the rest of the soaking wet men he commanded would wait for hours in the freezing cold and the dark preparing to carry out a mission. Every sound they heard made them tense and wonder if they would ever see another sunrise.

Some of those nights he didn't care what would happen to him. He was either too exhausted, too hungry, too injured, too cold or dying of thirst to give a rat's ass if he lived or died. But he did care for the men who looked to him to get them out of a tight spot. That was why he would stay awake in the cold and dark and wait for the sunrise.

The sunrise was the unspoken hope all the men clung to. There was something about dying in the dark that unnerved even the biggest and baddest dudes. As he had done many times during those long desperate nights years before in a filthy stinking foxhole, David refused to shut his eyes during that night in the garage, with Syd asleep on his shoulder.

CHAPTER 30

"SYD, HONEY, WAKE UP. IT'S morning," David said softly.

Seemingly wide awake in an instant, Syd said, "We need to call the police."

"We will, let's go home first and call them from there. We need to think about what we're going to say."

"Going to say? What's there to think about? Two of the nicest people we've ever known were murdered last night in their own home. What else *is* there to say?"

"We'll call the police later. I just want to get out of here. C'mon." David helped Syd to her feet and guided her to the garage door that led to the street. When he opened the door, he was shocked to see a man on the other side of it. Instinctively, David drew back the hammer he still had in his hand. Only when he recognized the face of Gino's eighty-three-year-old neighbor, Pauly, did he drop it to his side.

Pauly didn't see the hammer in David's hand because he was too busy with his morning chore of faithfully sweeping the sidewalk of his entire street. It was a short street, but it was still an entire damn street and he swept it with pride come rain or shine. When he finally looked up, he had a question. "You're that boy that drives for Gino, right?"

"Yes sir, I am."

"You the one that left this door open last night?"

"Yes, I guess I was."

"Well, it was a damn good thing I was up late and checkin' things out like I always do. I closed that door so Gino wouldn't get his butt robbed."

"Thanks Pauly. That was real thoughtful. By the way, did you see anyone else hanging around the garage last night?"

"Naw. Just saw a big fancy car drivin' by a few times. Looked like they was lookin' for an address."

"Could you tell what kind of car it was?"

"I think it was one of them Mercedes or Jap kinds. You know, big and fancy and black."

"Well, thanks again for closing that door Pauly, I'll make sure I won't leave it open again."

When David and Syd walked out of the garage together hand-in-hand, Pauly noticed and smiled. "Oh, didn't know you two was in there all night."

"Well, we think cabs are kind of romantic, don't you, Pauly?" Syd asked.

Pauly smiled at the thought. "Yeah, I remember some real good nights in cabs, yes young lady, I sure do."

As David and Syd walked down the street, Syd turned and waved. Pauly smiled even wider and waved back. Later at a Starbuck's, David announced, "I need a double espresso."

"Make it two."

After they ordered, David said, "I wonder how long it was before the bad guys left and we got there?"

"Couldn't have been too long. Do you think Gino told them you'd been driving the cab?"

"Most people would have. Especially with a knife at their throat. But Gino was a tough guy, former Marine. But the thing is Gino didn't know exactly where we lived. He knew we lived in the Village, but I think I used the address of that crap apartment I had when I was at NYU when I started driving for him years ago. I don't remember ever changing that address."

"They're looking for you, you know," Syd said.

"I would assume so."

"What's so damn important in that briefcase that they would kill three people?"

"You're the math major; maybe you can figure it out when we get home."

"Should we even go home?"

"I think we're safe from the cops even after they find Gino and Marie. I'm sure they'll question Pauly, and he'll tell them we were there last night and give them a description, but he doesn't know where we live either. But even so, we shouldn't go back to Gino's place for a while, that's for sure."

"Speaking of that, we need to call the police and tell them what happened. We can't wait any longer" Syd said.

"I know, I've been looking for a damn pay phone but can't find one. We can't use one of our cell phones; they will track it down."

"There's one down at that laundromat near the bus stop."

After Syd pulled a hood over her head and disguised her voice, she made the anonymous fifty-cent call alerting the police to check out Gino and Marie's house. Afterward David and Syd walked the eight blocks back toward their apartment. "Once the cops talk to Pauly, the whole damn city will be looking for you, Clyde." Syd said, citing criminal history.

"Don't forget, you're my accomplice, Bonnie." David said.

"At least I don't have cops from two big cities on my tail."

"Oh shit, I forgot about that DC cop."

"Yeah, you are forgetful at times. As the body count rises, it's hard to keep track."

"Let's go do some homework."

CHAPTER 31

BACK AT THEIR APARTMENT, DAVID spread the contents of the briefcase over the kitchen table. For nearly an hour, Syd pored over the files putting some of the material she read into separate piles. Finally, David asked, "Does any of this stuff make sense to you?"

"A lot of statistical algorithms and algebraic formulas. Pretty deep stuff."

"Does it look like anything people should be killing for?"

"I can't tell by looking at this kind of data, since I don't know how it was going to be used," Syd answered.

"I thought you were brilliant."

"I am, but these kinds of numbers and equations could be interpreted in a million different ways. I see references to polling data, the populations of congressional districts, several demographic studies, geographic analyses, probability ratios, and a bunch of other stuff. But how it was going to be used is the big unknown."

"James said that 'stat guys ruled the world.'"

"Well, depending on how the numbers were used, he could be right."

"What do you mean?"

"I mean that to some degree you can make statistics and data say anything you want them to say."

"But isn't that assuming those statistics and data are accurate?" David asked.

"Well obviously, but..."

"From what James told me, I got the impression he was saying that the people hearing all those numbers, people like you and me, even the media, were believing things that weren't true. That all of us were being manipulated, misled, and out-and-out lied to by those who were providing the basic information."

"You mean by the politicians and the political parties?" Syd asked.

"No, I think he was saying it went much higher than that."

"That sounds like that Deep State garbage. You don't believe that stuff, do you?"

"Frankly, I never gave it much thought. But think about it, what if there were a handful of organizations around the country that did in fact control all the statistics and all the data. Like you just said, they could make that stuff say anything they wanted it to say, whenever they wanted to say it," David said.

"Well, yeah, to a certain extent that's true, but that would only go so far. You could only skew those statistics and data so much."

"Not if you lied about the baseline data that was doled out in the first place. Then you could make people believe anything you wanted them to believe by serving up bogus statistics especially over a long period of time."

"To believe that all these econometric forecasting companies are fudging the numbers for a common political goal is taking a conspiracy theory to a whole new level," Syd said.

"I don't think it's only about a political agenda, I think it's also about these companies making a whole lot of cash by creating, then releasing these fake numbers to entities that could profit by knowing who will be president far in advance of anybody else."

"I wonder how many of those firms like James' there are in this country?" Syd asked.

For the next hour, Syd and David pored over their laptops. They searched Google and focused on companies that had anything to do with "forecasting," "econometrics," and "polling." They found over a hundred.

"I don't think the polling companies have any direct involvement with a conspiracy. They are just the customers of the forecasting firms and vendors to the media. They buy the results from those firms and then resell it to the media, who then reports it to the public," Syd said.

"It looks to me like most of these polling firms do their own research anyway," David said.

"Some do, some don't. Some just act as a middleman between the media and the forecasting firms."

"If you eliminate all the polling firms and small research firms, it looks to me like there are only four true econometric forecasting firms in the country that do the kind of work James described to me. One is in Boston, one in Palo Alto, one in Denver, and the one here in New York." David offered.

"I think you're right."

"So what's this all mean?"

"I don't know any more now than when we sat down. And I'm getting a headache looking at all these damn numbers," Syd said as she slumped back in her chair.

"We're missing something," David said.

"Like what?"

"We're missing whatever is in all these numbers that is important enough to justify three people being murdered."

Without any further discussion, Syd and David started over. They spent the next three hours looking at every interoffice memo, report, graph, and chart found in James' file. After a brief lunch and a walk around the block to clear their heads, they continued their work into the late afternoon.

At around 5:00, Syd sat up in her chair, silently reread a memo then said, "Looks like James was in charge of contacting large employers in major cities in the Northeast regarding their employment numbers for last year and hiring plans for next year."

"So?"

"It says here the four hundred companies James interviewed were roughly only 10% of the research done nationally."

"So?'

"So, then his company melded those results from all the other regions with statistics from the states and federal government regarding unemployment claims. Mix it all together and abracadabra you have an unemployment rate for February."

"Which was?" Asked David.

"Which according to James' research in his region was 10.5%."

"Then his region was much higher than the other regions since the national average was much lower. In fact, according to the media reports the national unemployment rate was 7.8%," David said as he finished off a slightly green banana.

"That means that most of the other regions should have had projected rates much lower than the 10.5% that James had in his region to bring the number down to 7.8%."

"Makes sense," David agreed.

"But they didn't. Most of the rates in the other regions were even higher than 10.5%" Syd said. "Does that mean they simply ignored the numbers guys like James found and threw out whatever number they wanted?"

"That's consistent with what James told me…basically that all the numbers the regional managers came up with were being manipulated."

"Would three people really be killed over 2.7 percentage points in an unemployment report?"

"James said it was all about trends. As long as the numbers were going in a positive direction, it was all good."

After a few more minutes of silent reading, David said, "Hey listen to this. It's a memo dated December 12, 2011, from someone with the initials C.S.R. The memo was marked confidential and addressed to 'Gentlemen': *A collective 9.9% for the February rate is unacceptable. The rate must be in the mid-7's in Feb. and show a slow but continual decline to the low 7's by Sept. The final drop will occur in Oct. and be released two weeks prior to the election. A drop from 7.1 to 6.8 will be sufficient according to our profiles and analytics.*

"Wonder why everything seemed to revolve around the unemployment rate?" Syd asked.

"There are other numbers relating to other things that were put in the media and helped sell a particular candidate, according to these files. But the unemployment rate, even if you have a job, seems to be a Cliff Notes snapshot of the economy for people who don't take the time or don't go beyond that single number to determine if things are going well or not."

"Then all these other reports were just for show," Syd said.

"Sure looks like it. Maybe that's why James was so amped up and obviously pissed off over this kind of thing. He would go out and do all the real reporting and get accurate numbers, and then whoever C.S.R. and the other 'Gentlemen' were would just manipulate those figures as they saw fit."

"I thought James worked for this company for over ten years. Why would he wait that long to get a conscience?"

"I don't know. But he was one of ten regional managers who would conduct this kind of research. Maybe he and they thought their individual numbers when blended with the other numbers would change the outcome of what they found in their individual regions. It's also interesting that James' name was not on the distribution list of that memo we saw."

"Maybe he wasn't supposed to see that memo. Maybe that memo showed him for the first time what was really going on behind the scenes," Syd said.

"Lots of 'maybes' there, but he didn't seem like the kind of guy who would fudge numbers for the sake of politics. He seemed like the Eagle Scout type of guy, if you know what I mean."

"So he wasn't like you?"

"No, he wasn't incredibly handsome, witty, well-endowed, and poor."

"I'm a little concerned how you determine that not 'well-endowed' part?"

"I did a little nerd profiling. Can't see that James had a big one."

"I dunno, some nerd guys can fool you."

"God, you were a slut."

"How about you, Mr. Stud Muffin?"

"That's different," David clarified.

"Really? How modern. Besides, you don't know a thing about my salacious past."

"I don't want to know unless it's really salacious," David rightly pointed out.

"Then you might be disappointed."

"Let's go get a pizza, I'm hungry," David said

"So, you'd rather get a pizza than hear about my sexual escapades?"

"Thin crust or thick crust?"

"Thin. And crispy." Syd said.

CHAPTER 32

ON THEIR WALK TO SAM'S Pizza three blocks away, Syd and David revisited what they had spent the day studying. "All the regional manager reports I read go to or come from someone with the initials C.S.R. Did you notice on most of those memos no one else was copied?"

"Yeah, I did. That means it's possible none of the ten regional managers knew what the other nine were reporting from month-to-month," Syd said.

"That's right, and I saw that each of those regional managers had to sign a confidentiality agreement not to share any of their individual findings with anyone else, including the other regional managers."

"That explains why they didn't compare notes or raise hell when a national report contradicted one of their regional reports."

As Syd and David approached Sam's, engrossed in their conversation, they didn't at first notice the dark colored Audi that drove slowly past them. Finally, David saw the black sedan and pulled Syd into the pizza place.

He thought he had seen three men in dark suits inside the car, but then again he had seen scores of dark colored Audi sedans recently and each time imagined all male occupants wore dark suits. He thought of an old song, "Paranoia strikes deep. Into your life it will creep."

After ordering a thin crust pizza with pepperoni, mushrooms, and tomatoes, Syd said, "So all that other polling about the economy, foreign policy, likability, the general economy, is really just a smokescreen."

"Looks like we are a single-issue population that doesn't even vote all that much. It's all about jobs and how much money someone can make."

"That's kind of cynical, isn't it?" Syd asked.

"Yep. But if someone comes on the scene and promises a better job and more money to a blue collar guy making less than he thinks he should, all the other issues go out the window. They just don't give a damn. The attitude is 'pay me a little more and I'll vote for you no matter what kind of asshole you are,'" David said.

"Then you have the group at the top end of the financial spectrum who just want tax cuts for their vote when they're already worth millions... or even billions. Damn, all this stuff is depressing as hell," Syd lamented.

"Yeah, it is. But I think that's what James was getting at. Like every other election, the next one will just hinge on jobs. If the unemployment number trends down as a percentage, Obama gets reelected. It's that simple because all the other issues are based directly or indirectly on unemployment or they are ignored by the voters despite what social issues they may scream and yell about. In short, everything but jobs is bullshit," David said as he began to destroy the thin crust pepperoni-laden delicacy.

"So, do you think James was killed because he found out the reported numbers were bogus?"

"It could certainly explain why people were chasing him and why he wanted to tell his story on C-Span." David said.

"I guess if some people thought those numbers were important enough it could also explain why Gino and Marie were killed too."

From the street, the sound of a blaring car horn made both Syd and David jump.

"David, if they thought those numbers were important enough to kill three people, and we have those numbers in our apartment, they may come after you."

"I've thought about that, but I don't think there is any way the bad guys can track me down. The cops either," David said, not at all convincingly.

"Okay, let's say we've solved the mystery of why James, Marie, and Gino were killed, and I'm not at all sure we have, what do we do with all this information? Who do we tell our story to? And who'd believe it?"

"I have no idea. Hell, I'm not ever sure I believe it," David said.

After several minutes and more pizza, Syd suggested, "How about that cop in DC?"

"Are you kidding? If he links James with Gino and Marie, I'll be wanted for suspicion of murder in several states if I'm not killed first by the bad guys in the Audi. I think the best plan is to lay low and keep quiet until this mess blows over."

"Blows over? We have information about three murders and potentially one of the biggest frauds ever perpetuated on the American public, and you want it to blow over? That doesn't sound like you."

"My hero days are over. I'm a writer now, something you said I should stick with. We aren't sure what we've seen is a crime or a fraud or anything else. Hell, we don't even know if James' murder is tied to Gino and Marie. It could all be just a coincidence. But most importantly, if I am in danger, so are you, and that is reason enough for me, and us, to keep quiet and move on."

For several minutes Syd and David were uncomfortably silent except for ordering two more glasses of red wine. Syd broke the tension by asking a question: "How about you writing a story about all this and sending it to the *New York Times* or *Washington Post*? You know, it could be "anonymous," or you could be one of those *unconfirmed sources* we hear about all the time."

"Unless I have some solid sources or proof of some sort, those papers won't print what I would write for fear of getting sued."

"Then how about writing a book?"

David pondered Syd's suggestion for several moments. "I guess that could work. But it would have to be nonfiction, and I've never written nonfiction."

"You're a damn writer, for God's sake, and a good one. Write it like a mystery but all true."

"We don't know it's all true," David said.

"We don't know it's not."

"I couldn't give too many details or someone reading it might be able to track us down."

"Just write it as a nonfiction book. Use a pseudonym, get it published, and then after it's out there and a hit, go on TV and announce your identity."

"What makes you think anyone would publish this story just because I write it?"

"Think about it. You're always looking for and dreaming up new stories. From what we know after only one day of reading these files, and what we know has already happened to James, Gino, and Marie, this could be the story you've always looked for. Something this explosive will surely be published by someone, someday," Syd said.

The fact was David needed little encouragement to leap feet first into such an intriguing project. However, he knew what such an endeavor would entail. He also knew the time such an effort would consume meant further erosion of their savings and more pressure on Syd to remain in a job she hated to be the sole income source for the two of them. "If I jump into this, it means "Little Sydney" or "Little David" will be put off a while longer, you know," David said.

"I think they will understand. Besides, it will give us a little more time to practice," Syd murmured as she got up and sat next to David in the booth.

"Okay, I'm in," David said, ready to immediately begin a rigid practice regimen.

CHAPTER 33

DAVID'S INITIAL EUPHORIA OF WRITING "The Story" quickly became an all-consuming obsession, tinged by a lingering fear that someone was waiting around the corner or in a darkened room to do to him and Syd what had been done to James, Gino and Marie. But in some way, that underlying tension, that specter of the unknown, that nagging fear made his writing better. It became sharper, more focused, more analytical; just better. In fact, he found himself, despite himself, writing for a cause. Writing for a reason far more important than just publishing a damn book.

He felt he was writing to right a wrong—for Gino, Marie, James, and even for his fellow citizens who didn't even know they were being screwed by a small group of people who had taken away something on which the country was founded. Something millions of men and women had died for since even before the Revolution. That idea pissed off David in a big way and that pissed-off-ness emerged in his writing.

Yet, he knew that if his story was to be believed by the press and the general public, he needed to write more than an opinion piece or an emotional tirade against those who had usurped a fundamental right and in the process killed three fellow Americans. He needed to provide as much definitive proof as he could, not so much to ultimately convict the bad guys, but to show the world what had occurred. Leave no doubt. No room for argument or political debate. He wanted to show people what had been taken from them when they weren't paying attention. Show them what could happen when they cared more about *Monday Night Football,* their Facebook page, Twitter account, or new smartphone than a right on which the damn country was founded. He knew that sounded a bit corny, even to him, but as he wrote, that emotion became real and tangible. It built up in him and became the drug that fueled his writing.

At the same time, as he wrote more and more, studied the files in James' briefcase, and did research on many of the things James had told him, he became disgusted with his fellow citizens. The fact that less than 50% of eligible Americans voted stunned him. He never knew that. But of even more concern was what he was learning about the 50% who did vote.

In short, most of the voters he analyzed were routinely bought. It was that simple. They were, for the most part, nothing more than *citizen whores* who were purchased by whomever promised lower taxes, or higher wages, or something else for nothing.

Then there were the politicians who well understood their empty-headed constituents. As a result, they made the same empty promises year after year, decade after decade, knowing their vacuous words would once again resonate with a new generation of "for sale" voters who would remain willingly ignorant of facts and devoid of any analytical thought. That ignorance would lead to the politicians being sent back to Washington over and over, which would allow them to build their personal net worth.

"I'm learning this is a sick process even if I can't prove that what James said is accurate." David told Syd over dinner two months into his "story."

"I'm surprised that you're surprised at what you're finding. Did you think it would be any different?

"One can always hope."

CHAPTER 34

THE ANNOUNCEMENT OF GINO AND Marie's murders became no more than a Page Six story in the *New York Post* and did not appear in the *New York Times* at all. If Pauly had given the police a description of Syd and David, they either never followed up or did not know where to look. The brutal murders were soon forgotten. It was the same with James' killing in DC. It was not covered in any detail by any of the major news outlets. It was just another unsolved crime among thousands in any given year in any big city.

Syd began to notice changes in David as he toiled over his story. Subtle at first, the changes became more pronounced as David sat in front of his computer in his home office for longer and longer periods of time. When he would return from the library after hours of research, he would be emotionally spent and irritable.

He stopped working out, had problems sleeping, began to grow a beard, and would have to be reminded by Syd that it had been three days since he last showered. He even stopped paying attention to sports on TV—a small thing to be sure, but indicative of the impact the story was having on the man she loved.

Of even greater concern for Syd was that David had lost interest in sex. He spent several nights a week sleeping in the guest room so he wouldn't keep Syd awake with his incessant typing that she could hear through the wall anyway. On more than one occasion, she thought about slipping into his room naked as a jaybird and "having her way" with David, but she decided to wait until he would be "into it" again. That would certainly be more fun.

More fun, but the waiting for David to return to being the *real* David was no less difficult for Syd. She understood and appreciated the time and work that he was putting into his writing. She knew he had latched onto this project with the same drive to conquer the beast that he had had during SEAL Hell Week. She realized the look on his face every morning when he would march off to his office and attack his computer was the same look she had seen after he had come off a twenty-mile run after no sleep for two days with little food or water.

Like David, Syd no longer looked at this project as a path to fame and fortune. It was far more than that. She knew the truth had to be told whether people believed it or not. The world needed to know that James, Marie, and Gino had died so David's story would NOT be told and that alone required someone to step up and tell the truth. Syd was proud of

David for taking on the heavy mantle of truth-teller.

Still, two months had been a long time to delay their quest for a return to their own special sexual higher ground. Particularly since the sex had been as spectacular three years into their marriage as it had been that first weekend they spent together in Manhattan.

It wasn't that she didn't believe in him or what he was trying to accomplish, but watching the love of her life obsess about putting the right words in the right order, almost to exclusion of everything else, was taking its toll on the team. His Pitbull-like preoccupation with this quasi-mistress had robbed them of the playfulness and sexual banter that had so often served as intoxicating foreplay. She missed the comradery. She missed the fun. She missed her best friend.

Most of David's waking hours were spent hammering the keyboard. He rarely left the apartment for any purpose other than trips to the library to learn more things he could hammer about. Syd realized that although taking on many of his day-to-day chores and not nagging him about the lack of marital bliss was helpful in its own way, she decided that if she couldn't beat 'em, and wasn't entirely sure she wanted to, she would join 'em.

When she offered to help, David was initially reluctant to come up for air—wary of breaking his concentration—but then he remembered he had *drafted her* all those years ago in part because she was, as he had admitted to himself on several occasions, smarter than he was. If she couldn't actually contribute, she certainly wasn't going to hurt the mission. They eventually got into a routine of Syd doing deep background research and proofing his drafts. They became an effective team, one that shared in executing a successful mission, if only in a roommate kind of way—for a while at least.

At a little after eight p.m. on election night 2012, David gazed blankly at the TV screen and heard: *"With a confirmation of a victory in Ohio, CNN can now declare that President Barack Obama has been reelected to his second term as the forty-fourth president of the United States. While votes will be coming in until tomorrow morning, it appears the president will win by four points, 51-47, over Mitt Romney."*

The announcement made David think back to that day in the cab with James. *"Obama, by four points."* He had stated, not as a prediction, but as a fact when answering David's question regarding who would win the election.

When David saw all the confetti and balloons being released on TV, saw all the smiling faces, funny hats, and the rest of it, he realized it was all a sham. He had always suspected it was all bullshit before, but after meeting James, reading the files, and doing some studying, all the celebrating seemed obscene to David. Like a group of people making fun of the Constitution. Making fun of what the country was built on. He thought of all the soldiers he had known who had been killed supposedly protecting the rights those people on TV were celebrating. In the end, it was utter bullshit. After that election-night announcement, David turned off the TV and wrote until three in the morning.

Over the next several months, David resumed his Bataan Death March approach to writing. He began to lose weight and looked increasingly haggard. He wore a favorite plaid shirt so long that Syd had to practically tear it off his back so she could wash it. He had also officially moved into the guest bedroom.

Less than two miles away, an impeccably dressed woman in an expensive suit had a pointed question for the two men who stood before her. "Why haven't you been able to find him?"

"There are no accurate records on the guy. We found where he used to live, but there was no forwarding address or phone number."

"What about his Social Security number? His boss must have had that."

"Looks like he may have been getting paid in cash."

"You mean with all the internet information available we can't find a single David Dawson in this entire city?"

"We have his name and some background info, but he doesn't own any real estate or have a listed phone number."

"I want him found."

"I understand, ma'am, but he seems to have gone underground, and I doubt he will cause any problems…"

"How the hell do you know that?"

"Well, I don't know for sure, but it seems like he's disappeared maybe he even left town after he heard what happened and…"

"Either you and your friend there find him, or I'll get someone who will. I don't like loose ends."

CHAPTER 35

David and Sydney's Apartment, February 2013

AS HE REREAD A 1974 *Time* magazine article about the Watergate break-in on his computer, he was interrupted by a call on his cell. "Hello," David said curtly.

"Hi David, my name's Vic Baker, hope I'm not bothering you. I was a neighbor and good friend of Gino and Marie's. I live across the street. I am also a retired attorney and used to help Gino on some of his business matters."

Taking on a more civil tone, David said, "Hi Vic, how can I help you?"

"Last week, I was asked by their estate to go through some of their papers and found a note from Gino regarding giving you and your wife some personal stuff here at the house. He had your phone number on the note, but when I checked your home address it was at NYU. Guess you've moved since then. If you like, I can package this stuff up and have a delivery service drop it off to you."

"Oh, well, okay. What kind of stuff is it?"

"Don't get too excited, it's just some knickknacks that Gino and Marie thought you guys might like someday. Doubt they knew it would be this soon."

"Okay, we're at 368 Hudson, second floor, unit #3. But I can always swing by and pick that stuff up if you like," David said.

"No worries, I pass by that way a couple times a week. Might be a few days but I'll call before I come over."

"Okay, thanks Vic. We sure do miss Gino and Marie." David said.

"Yeah, my wife Rose and I do too. They were good people. Just a damn shame what happened to them."

After a few more social niceties David said good-bye, hung up the phone, and immediately decided he needed a writer's nap to clear his brain.

Three hours later when Syd came through the front door, David was asleep on the couch. She carried with her a large stack of papers from work. She moved to the edge of the couch and sat down next to David. She tickled his nose with her scarf. He swatted her hand away and groaned.

"Hey, you degenerate, wake up. Where's dinner?"

David slowly opened his eyes. "I'm on the last chapter."

"Good, I want my man back."

"I think it's pretty good."

"I know it's good, honey. But Houston, we have a problem."

"What do ya mean?"

"Where's our damn dinner?" Syd asked, a look of pending starvation on her face.

"Oh, shit. I'm sorry, I fell asleep and… "

"Sounds like a Chinese night to me."

"I'll go. The usual?"

"Yeah, but get some wonton soup too." Syd said.

David rolled off the couch, kissed Syd on top of her head, grabbed his coat, and opened the door. Before he left, he turned to her, "Sweetie, I know I've been over the top on this damn book the last few months, but it means a lot to us. I'll be myself once this crazy thing is done. I'm sorry I've been such a major pain in the ass."

"That's okay as long as you don't become a bigger pain in the ass when you win the Pulitzer.

"Oh no, if I win the Pulitzer, I will be absolutely unbearable."

"Okay, fair enough. Don't forget the wonton. And by the way, your book is not crazy. Far from it."

"While I'm out, I'm gonna swing by a neighbor of Gino's, it's only half a block from China Cottage. He called and said Gino and Marie wanted us to have some stuff. He said he would drop it off, but I'll save him a trip."

"Think it's okay to head down that way?" Syd asked.

"Yeah, I think we're in the clear at this point."

"Okay. I'll take a shower and we can watch the Knicks while we eat."

"Sounds good. But don't overdress on my account when you're done."

"Ooh, baby. My boyfriend is back." Syd uttered in a pretty good Mae West voice.

David exited the apartment and walked the ten blocks to Gino's house. For the first time in months, he felt good. Like a weight was off his shoulders. While he had one chapter left, he knew the ending like the back of his hand and wanted to get the damn book done and enjoy life again. Enjoy his wife again and make things up to her. Lots of things. He remembered the wonton.

CHAPTER 36

DAVID KNOCKED ON WHAT HE thought was Vic's door across the street from Gino's, but there was no answer. He knocked again and was about to leave when Pauly, Gino's former street-sweeping octogenarian neighbor, stopped him with a bit of information. "No one lives there, boy. That place has been locked up tighter than a drum for over a year now."

"Hi, Pauly. I just stopped over to see if I could catch up with a neighbor of Gino's named Vic. He said he had some things Gino wanted us to have."

"Ain't no Vic around here. I know everybody, and there ain't no Vic in this neighborhood." Pauly said definitively.

"Oh really? He just called me today and said he was gonna drop off some things at my place, and I figured I'd save him a trip."

"Like I said, ain't no Vic around here, but there was some men in a fancy car snoopin' around a few times today. Maybe one of them is that Vic guy."

"When was the last time that car was here?" David asked, deathly afraid of the answer.

"Hell, you just missed them, they was here no more than fifteen minutes ago."

CHAPTER 37

BEFORE SYDNEY ENTERED THE SHOWER, she turned on her CD player in the bathroom so she could sing along with Adele and get squeaky clean at the same time. She really felt in her heart that if something bad happened to Adele, she could step right in and her fans would never know the difference in their voices. Since she really liked Adele, she didn't want anything bad to happen to her, but just in case, she was ready to serve if drafted.

Given the shower noise, shampoo in her ears, and her harmonizing with Adele, Syd didn't hear anything when someone turned the front-door handle. Whoever tried the handle tried it two more times, but the extra lock that David had installed a few months earlier held.

Moments after the attempts to open the door in a somewhat dignified manner failed, the door frame was splintered with the help of small crowbar, and the door flew open. This time Syd thought she heard something and shut off the water. She listened intently, but there was no further sound. When she turned off the overhead fan, she listened again. "David?"

When there was no reply, she turned the water back on and continued her shower and her duet with Adele. After she rinsed the conditioner out of her hair, she stepped out of the shower, dried off and used the hair dryer for a few minutes.

Hoping for the best, she applied a bit of makeup and just a touch of perfume in vital spots in anticipation of a bit of celebrating in the biblical sense with her best guy. After she was done, she wrapped a large yellow towel around herself, opened the bathroom door and moved into the hallway.

When she stepped from the hallway into the bedroom, she was grabbed from behind by a very large man in a dark blue suit. He placed one hand around her neck, and the other held a large serrated knife that he placed next to her cheek. A second man in a black cashmere turtleneck sweater named John Mercer laid back casually on her bed and watched the activity in front of him, a satisfied grin on his face.

"My dear, what a truly unexpected surprise. You must be the elusive David's lovely wife Sydney. Who would think a cab driver could score such a beautiful woman?"

"He's not here," Syd said calmly.

"He never seems to be anywhere, that husband of yours. Very hard to catch up with him and I must admit we have tried to locate your elusive cab driver for months. When do you expect the wandering Mr. David to be home, my dear?"

"I don't know. He went out. Not sure where he went."

"Hard to understand why a man would leave such a beautiful woman all alone. If I was David, I would spend all my time with such a lovely young lady. You wouldn't mind if we have a better look at you, would you?"

The man with the knife to Sydney's face reached down and pulled off her yellow towel. She stood naked in front of the two men, her eyes riveted on Mercer who asked, "Is it true that a beautiful woman like you is a CPA?" He asked. "With a face and figure like that, you should be in the movies not preparing tax returns. Big Rico, don't you think the beautiful Sydney here should be in the movies?"

Big Rico uttered something that was more of a low moan than a real response to Mercer's question. As he looked down at Sydney, his face flushed, his eyes bulged, and his wide grin exposed uneven yellow teeth. Finally, he said, "I wanna do stuff to her."

"Of course you do, Big Rico, and we'll certainly get around to that soon enough. But before we do, we need to ask Sydney here a few questions. Like, where's your husband, sweetie?"

Syd refused to answer but never took her gaze off Mercer.

"C'mon honey, we just need to talk to David about some files of ours we know he has, and as soon as he gives us those files, we'll be out of here in no time."

Again Syd refused to answer, her stare continuing to bore into the man on her bed whose own grin had widened.

"Of course, if you give us those files right now, we would leave this very minute," Mercer said.

"Before we fuck her?" Big Rico asked with obvious disappointment.

"I have no idea about any files."

"Well then, I'm afraid your husband may be hiding something from you, Sydney."

"Big Rico, would you like to touch the lady who doesn't know anything about our files? If so, feel free to do so."

As he held the knife to Syd's throat, Big Rico reached down and began to massage Sydney's left breast with his left hand.

"Does that feel good to you, Sydney?" Mercer asked. "If so, I'll bet I can get my large friend there to do even more things you might like."

"They're real, boss." Big Rico said, hardly able to contain his unbridled glee.

Sydney gave serious thought to driving the palm of her left hand upward, breaking Big Rico's nose and ramming it into his brain. She also considered a shot to his throat that would certainly disable the fat fuck, but she didn't know if the asshole on the bed was armed although she suspected he was. Relying on years of training, she decided she needed more information. She needed to be calm and patient and wait for an opening.

"Are you recalling any files at this point, Sydney?"

"David never mentioned any files to me," Sydney said flatly.

"Is there anything else you would like to touch, Big Rico?"

"Yeah, I want to touch her…you know, down there."

"Then go ahead, Big Rico, go ahead and touch her *down there*, I can tell Sydney there is really getting into you."

Big Rico moved his thick hands down between Sydney's legs and fondled her with an even larger grin on his face. Sydney remained motionless and stared directly into Mercer's eyes. With a smile on his face, he asked, "C'mon honey, where's that lover boy of yours?"

Ignoring Big Rico's clumsy groping, Sydney said in flat monotone, "He's working tonight; he won't be home till morning."

"Another night of driving a cab to make a living, huh?" Mercer asked.

Syd nodded. She also thought she saw a pistol in a shoulder holster that Mercer was wearing under his left arm. If she could in fact get free of the three-hundred-pound Neanderthal who was annoying her with his clumsy fondling, she would be able to go for Mercer before he could unholster his weapon.

"Well then, we will just have to wait until he comes home, so we can have a chat with him. But in the meantime, we might as well have some fun while we do. We wouldn't want you to get bored."

"Big Rico, please bring Sydney over here so she and I can get better acquainted."

"How come you get to go first?"

"Seniority, my friend. Plus a knowledge and appreciation of the female form. Most importantly, I understand the needs of a beautiful young woman like Sydney here."

"Can I still fuck her too?"

"Of course, my impatient friend, of course. But for now just watch and learn."

Sydney grimaced and struggled against the squat three-hundred-pound man in the blue suit. He grinned and pushed her onto the bed into Mercer's arms.

As the fifty-something graying man held her, he offered Syd some advice. "Now Sydney, this *is* going to happen no matter what you do. First, I am going to fuck you after you suck my dick. Then Big Rico is going to fuck you after you suck his dick. So please, for your sake, just accept the inevitable. The fact is, you might even like it if you just let it happen and not make a big fuss. You wouldn't have to tell your favorite cab driver you enjoyed it. It would be between just the two of us and of course Big Rico there, but he won't tell our secret. That's right, isn't it, Big Rico? You won't tell the cabbie his little wife liked getting fucked by two guys while he's driving his yellow cab."

"I won't tell", Big Rico said as he rubbed his crotch in anticipation.

"See, Big Rico won't tell and I won't tell, so you can just lay back, go with the flow and enjoy, enjoy, enjoy. You know what I mean? Of course, if you don't lay back and go with the flow, Big Rico there might just use his big knife or some other tools he has in ways you may not like. I'd hate to see that pretty face or any of those other beautiful body parts of yours get all cut up. That would be such a waste. Do you understand?"

CHAPTER 38

AS SOON HE HEARD PAULY describe the big black Audi, David sprinted down the street toward his apartment. He crossed against lights, twice almost getting hit by cars that blared their horns at the crazy guy with a death wish. He ran as fast as he could, his feet scarcely touching the ground. When he arrived at his apartment building, he rushed up the first flight of stairs in two long steps. On the second floor at the end of the hall, he saw that his front door was slightly off kilter. Wood splinters were scattered on the carpet in front of the door.

He resisted the urge to immediately burst into the living room not knowing where his enemy was located or how well armed he was. Most importantly, he did not know where Sydney was. Would his blind attack save her or end up killing her?

He moved next to the front door, tried to control his heavy breathing, then peered inside to determine if he could see or hear anything emanating from the apartment. All he heard was a low indistinct murmur of conversation, but he couldn't see directly into the bedroom. Then he heard men's voices and laughter.

Through the narrow crack of the door that was slightly separated from the jamb, he could see into the hallway that led into the bathroom. On the floor he saw a yellow bath towel. He gritted his teeth and felt his pulse pound. He silently pushed open the front door and heard men laughing again, this time louder. He thought he could hear Syd's voice, calm and controlled.

He again resisted the overwhelming urge to barge into the bedroom and take his chances. But from deep inside, years of training and discipline took over. He forced his pulse to slow. He forced himself to think. He made himself aware of his surroundings and considered his options. He evaluated the enemy.

He moved with his back against the living room wall and kept his eyes on the bedroom door. When he reached the antique mahogany desk in the corner, he silently opened a side drawer and pulled out a .38 revolver.

There was more men's laughter from the bedroom. David again had to rein in his primal instincts. He held his breath as he moved onto the black area rug behind the dining room table and inched his way toward the bedroom.

Through the crack created by the area near the hinges of the door, he saw the back of a very large man in a suit who stood next to the bed with a huge knife in his hand. He was looking down at Syd and another man in a turtleneck sweater who was on the bed fondling and kissing her neck and breasts. He took her hand and put it on his penis, which he had conveniently removed from his pants. Syd stared blankly up at the ceiling, her face emotionless.

Just as Mercer began to push Syd's head down, David came around from the back of the door and aimed the .38 squarely between Mercer's eyes, which suddenly got very wide. David knew that from that range he couldn't miss the son of a bitch.

Mercer also knew David couldn't miss so he simply waited for what was to come and had the slightest touch of resignation on his face. David, on the other hand, had a slight grin on his face. He pulled the trigger.

Instead of the anticipated "bang," there was a disturbing, almost embarrassing "click." The sound a .38 caliber pistol makes when it has no bullets. That sound made Mercer and Big Rico turn their undivided attention to David.

The look on Mercer's face had morphed from fear to one of immense relief. The look on Big Rico's face as he turned to David was a different kind of look. Like when someone is looking forward to engaging in a fun pastime.

David saw that look on Big Rico's face and was not encouraged. Nor was he inspired by the sight of the huge serrated knife that David now saw up close and personal. Particularly the gleaming edge. Big Rico, on the other hand, was thoroughly enjoying the moment based on his size and weapon advantage over a smaller, unarmed, and clearly frightened opponent. With a smile on his face, Big Rico playfully flipped the gigantic knife around in his right hand for what appeared to be dramatic effect.

It was very clear that David was not at all enjoying the moment given the sudden and unforeseen change in circumstances. He slowly backed out of the bedroom with a look of utter fear and helplessness on his face. Seeing David's rising level of fear made Big Rico's smile even wider. He was going to enjoy this.

David looked desperately around the living room for something, anything, to use as a weapon. He found nothing. Big Rico came out of the bedroom into the living room and moved ever closer to David. Then quite suddenly David stopped retreating. He no longer seemed afraid. He even smiled at Big Rico, which confused the large fellow quite a bit.

When David smiled, Sydney saw that smile as her signal. She reached out and touched someone. But not in a good way. With her left hand she grabbed Mercer's balls and used the dreaded "twist and pull" move to perfection. This elicited a wail of pain from him that was ironically, and under the circumstances, almost girl-like in tone.

She followed that move up with two quick jabs with the palm of her right hand into Mercer's face, the second of which broke his nose. Even after he tried to fight back and hit Syd in the side of her head with his fist, she hung on to his balls tenaciously like an incensed Pitbull, much to the dismay of Mercer and his throbbing scrotum. She then fired two more punches into Mercer's face, breaking the orbit of his right eye.

Before Big Rico could respond to what was happening on the bed, David executed a perfect spin move and brought his right foot around and up in less than a half a second and broke Big Rico's left jaw in three places.

At the same instant Syd used her right hand to pull Mercer's revolver from its holster and in a single motion released her grip on his balls then shot them off along with his no longer erect penis with a single shot.

As the gunshot reverberated in the small bedroom, David unleashed a powerful blow with an opened right hand directly below his left ear that broke Big Rico's neck. With his eyes open wide in shock, Big Rico began a slow-motion collapse to the floor like a California redwood.

As the already dead Big Rico pirouetted toward the carpet, Syd removed all doubt by firing a second shot that caught the big guy in the right temple, removing significant amount of brain matter. As he fell, David grabbed the knife from his hand and with perfect form threw it at Mercer a millisecond after Syd fired at Big Rico. The knife sliced through Mercer's throat, coming out on the opposite side from where it had entered. Blood from the balls/penis-removing bullet, and the jugular-slicing knife spewed over the white bedsheets and onto Syd's face.

Through it all, Mercer was not quite dead and gamely tried to speak although he was admittedly having some difficulty in that regard. David approached the bleeding, gagging, ball-less, penis-less man and had a question. "Who do you work for, asshole?" Not getting a satisfactory response, David repeated himself, "I said, who do you work for, you fucking asshole?"

"Maybe if you took that knife out of his throat, he'd tell you." Syd helpfully suggested as she simultaneously wiped blood from her face and tried to open a direct line of communication between the two men.

When Mercer finally and inevitably collapsed back on the bed, with his eyes wide open in death and a gurgling/hissing sound emanating from his throat, it was clear he would not be answering any more questions.

For several seconds David continued to shake in rage with a look on his face that Syd had seen only once before. Then as if a switch was turned off, he looked at then embraced Syd and asked, "Are you okay, honey?"

"I think so. How about you?"

"I'm fine." David said.

"Sweetie, I'm really sorry I took the bullets out of the gun. I was afraid you might hurt yourself," Syd explained.

"Why have a damn gun in the house with no…"

"I know, I know. Next time. Are you sure you're okay, honey?"

"Yeah, I'm good. Damn, who were these guys?"

"Obviously the ones who killed Gino and Marie," Syd concluded.

"This was all my fault. I was such an idiot. I gave them our address. What the hell was I thinking?" David admitted.

"Fuck 'em. Does this mean you forgot my wonton?"

CHAPTER 39

BEFORE HE BECAME A COP, New York City Detective Ernie Simmons had started out on the wrong side of the law as a member of a tough all-black gang in the Bronx called The Vipers. The deep scars on his face and body, reminders of the many fights he had survived over the years, gave him a glowering and menacing look of someone you didn't want to mess with.

His life would have most likely ended early as a gang member except for his good fortune to have almost died from a knife wound and nearly had his left kidney removed.

While he was in the hospital recovering from the wound that left a jagged nine inch scar on his side, he was visited by a coach of the high school football team who suggested that at six foot four, 240 pounds, Ernie might like playing football a bit more than getting stabbed every other week. After some thought, Ernie concluded that might not be such a bad idea.

After he quit the gang and returned to high school, he not only played and starred on the football and basketball teams, he also started to work on his grades and ended up getting a combined athletic and academic scholarship to Rutgers University where he studied criminal justice. He had thought about law school but decided he would probably make a lousy attorney and besides, he hated attorneys. So he decided to join the Marines for a while to sort out what he would do with the rest of his life.

After he returned from the service, he surprised everyone who knew him when he announced he wanted to become a cop. "Ernie a cop?" was the question nearly everyone who knew him had asked. He surprised them even more when he was accepted into the New York City Police Academy.

After finishing near the top of his graduating class, he joined the force as a rookie cop and for two years walked the beat back on his old turf in the Bronx. During that period, he saw many of his old gang buddies end up in body bags and realized how close he had come to the same fate.

After twenty-five years on the force, Ernie had worked his way up the ladder to chief detective and had over that period of time seen it all. More than once. So seeing two dead guys in an apartment, one with a knife stuck in his throat, wasn't something that was going to keep him awake at night. The only thing unusual about this case was how an average size writer and his smallish wife got the drop on two armed thugs, one of who looked like a NY Giants defensive tackle.

After the bodies were photographed, tagged, bagged, then removed from the apartment, Ernie sat at the dining room table with David and Syd, both of whom seemed unusually calm despite what had happened to them only a couple hours before. Ernie pushed aside some Chinese food containers, including some wonton soup that had been delivered during his investigation, and began to scribble notes in his notebook. He looked disinterested and bored.

Finally, he looked up at David and asked, "Ever see these guys before?"

"No, not exactly."

"What the hell does 'not exactly' mean?"

"If you find a black Audi S-8 around here, I bet it belongs to them. If so, I may have seen them in DC some few months ago."

"DC?"

Over the next hour, David told the detective what had happened with James in DC and how he thought that incident was directly related to Gino and Marie being murdered. He told him everything. Almost.

"So what do you think they were after? Why did they kill the guy in DC, your boss and his wife, then come after you guys?"

"Damned if I know. Maybe they thought there was something in the cab that wasn't there. Maybe James in DC took whatever they were after and hid it somewhere down there. I don't know. Maybe they were just fucking crazy," David said.

Ernie sat back in his chair and spent a few moments going over his notes. "You guys got a permit for that gun?"

"It's in the desk drawer. Want to see it?" Sydney said.

"Not if it's really there."

"It's there."

"Next to the bullets?" David asked.

Sydney gave David the finger, which Ernie pretended not to see.

"Which one of you stabbed the one on the bed?'"

"I didn't exactly stab him."

"How did he get a twelve-inch knife stuck in his throat, fall on it?"

"I threw it."

"You threw that damned knife?" Ernie asked.

"I got a pretty good arm. Pitched in college."

"How did you take care of the other one?"

"Spinning leg kick."

"Learn that in college too?"

"I took karate classes in the Navy."

"Bet you got pretty good grades in those classes."

"Pretty good."

"Sydney, did they…"

"No, they didn't," she said.

"That's good. God knows where they've been."

"I wanted to shoot them," Sydney said.

"Were you going to throw the bullets at them?" David asked.

Another finger. Ernie saw that one and choked back a laugh. He decided he liked Syd. Wasn't so sure about David.

Ernie went over his notes one last time, then closed his notebook. "You guys were real lucky. I'm gonna get hold of that detective down in DC and see what he knows. He and I may want to talk to both of you again at some point so don't leave town without contacting me."

"Okay, just let us know. We're going to move into a hotel for a while until this place is cleaned up. Just use my cell if you need us," David said.

Ernie nodded, got up and motioned for the other policemen to leave the apartment. "Night, folks," he said.

After Ernie left, David and Syd sat silently at the dining room table for nearly five minutes.

David finally said, "You realize we can never come back here again. There will be others coming after us."

"Get that damn book done."

CHAPTER 40

OVER THE NEXT TWO WEEKS they lived in a Residence Inn secured with Sydney's mother's Visa. Finally, and at long last, David, with Sydney's editing help, finished his damn book.

During that time they never spoke of what had happened in their apartment. Instead they survived on AMC flicks, pizza, gallons of coffee, and expectation. Sort of like buying a lottery ticket with a gazillion-dollar jackpot.

After some chicken burritos at lunch, David made an unexpected announcement. "I want you to take a month off work and go visit your parents in Florida."

He received an unexpected response. "Okay," Sydney said.

They both agreed it would be safer if Sydney left town while David remained in the New York area and shopped his book to publishers, editors, and agents. She knew he would be a nervous wreck leaving her alone each day, even if she was at work.

At LaGuardia two days later, David kissed Sydney goodbye at the curb. "Before you leave, I want to tell you how damn scared I was I had lost you back at... you know."

"It's going to take more than two large armed men for you to get rid of me. I'm here for the duration, mister."

"I love the hell out of you." David said as he held Sydney as close as LaGuardia airport security would allow.

"I love you too, and I'm going to miss you, big boy."

"Okay sailor, I'll let you know what happens with the agents and editors. I'm doing a bunch of pitches to some small publishers too, plus mailing a couple dozen query letters this week. We'll get something."

"People need to know what's happening, David. They have to know."

Sydney stayed at the curb until David's cab had disappeared around the corner of the terminal building.

CHAPTER 41

Manhattan

THE DAY AFTER SYDNEY LEFT New York, David was up at five thirty and at Kinko's by seven. He printed thirty copies of the first twenty-five pages of his manuscript along with a synopsis of his story and a cover letter. He stuffed the twenty-five packages into envelopes and by early afternoon was on the streets of Manhattan dropping off those packages to agents, editors and publishers.

By late afternoon that first day he had also called the *New York Times*, *New York Post*, *Washington Post*, *Philadelphia Inquirer*, and a few other rags and asked for a meeting to discuss a "headline news story." Some told him to fuck off nicely. Some just told him to fuck off.

He didn't really expect an editor of a publishing company or even an agent to actually come out and talk to him when he dropped off a package. On the other hand, he felt an in-person cold call where someone could maybe attach his package with his face was better than dropping a bunch of envelopes in the mail and hoping for the best.

A week later, David again arose early and at 9 a.m. began the process of calling back the agents and publishers he had left packages with. By noon, he had gotten twenty-three "Sorry, it's not for us" responses. Of the seven remaining, five said, "Give us a few weeks/months and we'll get back to you if we think we can sell this." One publisher said they "might have interest" but could not see him for a week. One never bothered to respond to his package or his call.

After the last call, David felt a sense of desperation he had never felt before. Some people may have identified the emotion as fear. But he had experienced physical fear in battle, and this was not that. It was, instead, a paralyzing helplessness he had never known in his life.

What he confronted at that moment, as he sat on the edge of his hotel room bed, was not an opponent he could fight and defeat with a knife or his fists. He felt as if he was trying to fight dangerous enemies in a dark room without a weapon.

But his utter defenselessness at that moment was not about him or about his story and book being ignored by seemingly everyone in New York; it was the recognition that everything that he and Syd had discovered in those damn files had spiraled out of control.

Five people had already died over what they had uncovered. His wife had been attacked by murderers, the government of the country he loved was quite possibly a sham, his career was in a shambles, and it was likely they were both being stalked like prey by those he had learned of and written about.

If his book was not released, then the secrets he and Syd had discovered would continue, and the American public would never learn how they were being deceived. They would continue to foolishly believe that their vote meant something.

Yet if lighting struck, and his book was somehow published, it seemed certain that he and Syd would be on someone's hit list somewhere, maybe forever, once the story got out. David was beginning to see it as a lose/lose situation.

If it was only him in the crosshairs, David could handle that. He was more than willing to defend himself, to fight—hell, he *wanted* to fight, just like during his hand-to-hand battles in close quarters when he was a SEAL.

But at that moment on the edge of that hotel bed, the fear he felt was all about Syd. What those files had done to her life. For God's sake, he had almost lost Syd, and her life had been turned upside down over his quixotic quest to tell a damn story.

He felt like he was flailing in the dark trying to hit unseen assailants who lay in wait ready to jump out at any moment from the darkness. Or worse, the people wouldn't fight, they wouldn't even respond to him. They would just wait, letting him stew and twist in the darkness.

While David felt defenseless, he didn't panic. But he almost did. Like being on your stomach as you try to crawl through a tight space in a narrow, damp cave and for just three seconds, you feel the terror of being utterly and completely stuck in the darkness. You feel the unemotional embrace of cold rock all around you. You are unable to move forward or backward or side to side. Your arms and legs are helpless. Sweat erupts all over your body, your heart pounds. You are breathing yet suffocating at the same time. You feel an approaching terror you've never felt before.

Then the person who thinks they're stuck in the cave relaxes. They fight through the terror by using their brain and, slowly but surely, they inch their way through the narrow space and move on. They do survive after all. But that memory of utter mindless terror never goes away. They will remember those three seconds for the rest of their lives. David would always remember that feeling, that day on the edge of the bed in the Residence Inn.

At that moment, he also wanted to be with Sydney more than he ever had since he had known her. Just talk to her. But he couldn't bring himself to call her and share more bad news. More failure.

He decided Syd deserved more than that. He loved her enough to want her to be happy and free of the life he had created for her with his indulgence to write. For having the audacity to think people would want to read what came out of his fucked-up brain. For allowing Sydney to be swallowed up in what had become not only a life built on his failure, but how his insistence on writing had created a situation where she was in danger every day. All this because he wanted to write a goddamn book based on what he had found in the back of his cab. Something that would likely be forgotten in a month, even if it were ever published. What the fuck had he been thinking?

As David's self-pity and self-recrimination was reaching "jumping off a tall building" proportions, his cell phone rang. The call was from an assistant to the senior editor of Thompson and Thompson Publishing, one of the publishers David had delivered a package to. The one who had not responded. The young lady said her boss, George Steberl, was anxious to meet with him and discuss his story and would David be available to come to their office at the end of the week?

After a time was set for the meeting, David's euphoria reached dangerous levels. While still two days away, he began rehearsing in his head how he would tell his story. He wondered what he should wear to the meeting. Should he go beard or no beard? Should his attitude in front of the editor be aloof or desperate? Or maybe desperately aloof?

When he called Sydney, he tried his best to downplay the meeting. "Probably just a waste of time" he had said. Syd knew better. She could see through David's attempt to manage expectations. She could sense his attempt to control his excitement and anticipation.

She was also afraid for David. She understood what he was going through given both the personal impact his quest for a writing career had had on both their lives, but also the toll this specific story had taken on him.

His urgency to have his story out there was more than just a writer getting rich and famous. It was the fact that the country both of them had served in the Navy was being manipulated by a handful of number crunchers desperate enough to kill as many people as necessary to keep David's story from the pages of *The New York Times*.

CHAPTER 42

THE NIGHT BEFORE HIS MEETING with Thompson and Thompson, David couldn't sleep. Instead he watched TV all night. He finally dozed off around 5 a.m. When he woke up two hours later with the remote still in his hand, he felt like shit. After a quick shower and a breakfast of Cheerios and toast, he still felt like shit, but he walked to the offices of Thompson and Thompson on East 47th Street.

For some reason, David knew this was it. This was *the* meeting. One way or the other. After this meeting he would either be a writer for rest of his life, or he wouldn't. He would either warn the country of what was happening to it every election day, or it would continue on its path of blind acceptance of numbers that would create whatever candidate the "stats men" wanted.

Thompson and Thompson at least looked like what a publisher's office should look like. It had dark wood paneling, large overstuffed chairs and couch, with Chippendale furnishings. Standing there, waiting for the receptionist to get off the phone, David felt like a real writer.

"May I help you?" the receptionist asked with a friendly smile.

"Yes, I have a lunch appointment with Mr. Steberl."

"Mr. Dawson?"

"Yes, David Dawson."

"I'm so sorry, we tried to call you this morning, but Mr. Steberl is out sick today and won't be able to make your lunch. However, he has arranged for you to meet with his assistant, Miss Adams."

For a full three and a half seconds, David looked down at the still smiling receptionist and smiled back. But what he really wanted to do was to jump up and down like a six year old who has been told he had missed the ice cream truck. He wanted to wail, "You've got to be fucking kidding me!" He wanted to pound the glass that separated him from the smiling receptionist. He wanted to tell her he hoped good old Mr. Steberl had shingles or a couple of kidney stones, or the clap. Instead, he held his own smile, remembered his SEAL training class on composure and said, "That would be perfectly fine, thank you so much."

At 11:45 David was led to the small, cramped office cubicle of Steberl's assistant. Her name was Tiffany. *Of course it was*, he thought. Tiffany looked like she was thirteen. Although David figured she was at least twenty-three given her diploma in literature from Fordham, which hung over her desk along with several pictures of her holding her white toy poodle. *Of course.*

Before she greeted David, Tiffany put on her red framed glasses, moved some papers around her cubicle, checked her email, took out her watch, and placed it in front of her on a stack of unread manuscripts. "I have a lunch appointment at noon."

"It's ten till."

"Then perhaps we should work quickly." Tiffany explained not understanding the potential physical risk of her comments.

Holding in primitive urges, David instead began his story. "Okay, Tiffany, here's the deal; nine months ago I drove this guy to DC who had found out all the statistics the media relies on from all these econometric groups is bullshit, all bogus, and further that all the elections from 1952 until now have been predetermined by a small group of rich guys, and the elections won based on these bogus numbers. The guy who told me this story was murdered an hour later."

As David's anger rose, he spoke faster and louder. He was frustrated at the assistant across from him and pissed he'd wasted half a day coming downtown for a ten-minute pitch to a fucking *assistant.*

"Then my boss and his wife were killed by the same bad guys because the bad guys thought they had the briefcase which contained that info that proved the dead guys' story, but in reality I had that information, and with the help of my wife, we figured out the truth; so the bad guys came after me and my wife, but I killed both of them protecting my wife who was on the bed naked with one of the bad guys, although she claimed she was in complete control of the situation, truth is, she had to grab his balls and squeeze them like hell; then I karate kicked one guy and broke his neck and stabbed the other one in the neck with a big fucking knife; then the cops came and said we had done nothing wrong since the bad guys had broken into our apartment and tried to kill us, so, in review Tiffany, this is a story about how our Constitution has been subverted by a group of rich guys and how these guys will kill anyone who tries to uncover this silent government overthrow; it's a story filled with intrigue, murder, money, subterfuge, some ball grabbing, a cool car, and is a story I think would become a *New York Times* best seller, make this company a shit load of money, and turn me into a literary giant. *That's my* fucking story, Tiffany."

After his high-speed, high-volume pitch/rant/vent, David looked at his watch and said, "Tiffany, we still have six minutes before your lunch."

After he spoke, the young assistant looked slack-jawed and in awe at hearing such an amazing story and sat in silence for several moments.

"Did you say this is nonfiction?"

"Yes. It's all true. Every damn word of it."

Tiffany looked unsure as to what to do next. "Like, that is such an amazing story. Oh, my God, like I can't wait to read it! I need to speak with our senior editor, Mr. Steberl's boss right now. Please wait here, don't go away now, I'll be right back."

When Tiffany left the room, David pounded his fist into his palm and uttered a guttural "Yes!" under his breath. David wanted to call Syd at that very moment. He wanted to share that moment with her. He wanted to share with her the victory over literary tyranny and oppression. In less than two minutes Tiffany returned to the small office with an announcement.

"Sorry, our senior editor said it's not for us, but thank you so much for coming in."

CHAPTER 43

David and Sydney's Apartment

DAVID WASN'T A QUITTER. BUT he was a realist. After his meeting at Thompson and Thompson, he had gotten drunk on his ass. In fact, he stayed reasonably drunk for two days. It felt good. But then he sobered up, and it felt bad. Without speaking to Syd in detail, other than to tell her his last meeting was another no, he had made a decision. It was at long last time to move on.

He had given writing a chance and he had utterly, completely, and totally failed. There was no other way to look at it. If he couldn't sell this latest story, it wasn't going to happen. The fact that some people said he was a talented writer was bullshit. Had he been any good he would have been published and been on several talk shows by now and living in California negotiating with movie studios.

Instead David sat at his desk at their old apartment with moving boxes all around him. The damage and blood stains caused by Big Rico and Turtleneck had been repaired and cleaned, and Syd had agreed that perhaps a career and location change was in fact a good idea for both of them.

The plan was that David would wrap up things in New York in a few days, come down to Florida and stay with her parents. Then he and Syd would plan out the rest of their lives in sunshine with the help of Mai Tais on the beach, until their savings ran out.

When the phone rang, David assumed it was a call from Syd, and answered, "What's up, hot stuff?"

"David, this is Detective Robert Casey from the Washington DC, Homicide Department. We spoke briefly several months ago about the murder of Dr. McDowell at the Hay Adams."

"Yes, we did, but I didn't do it, and how did you get my number?"

Ignoring David's question, Casey said, "Never thought you did. But I'd like to come to New York and take your statement just so we can put a ribbon on this investigation."

"The guys who killed the doctor killed my friends and tried to kill my wife and me."

"Yes, we know that. I spoke with the detective in New York. We have DNA matches from all three crime scenes and…"

"Then why come up here?" David asked. "Is this about leaving the scene of a crime stuff?"

"No, nothing like that, we understand there were some extenuating circumstances. Like I said, it's just a formality, but I can't force you to meet with me if you don't want to since you're not a suspect. It would just make my life a little easier, that's all."

After pondering if he really wanted to make the detective's life easier, David said, "Okay, I'll meet you at the Friday's in Penn Station tomorrow at four. Easy in and easy out for you."

"Thanks, I appreciate that. See you then."

"Hey, how will I recognize you?"

"Don't worry, the cops in New York sent me your photo, I'll recognize you."

After he hung up with Casey, David returned to the work of opening a couple more rejection letters he had received from various agents and editors. He found even more email rejections on his computer that he had originally copied and saved for some perverse reason. As if it was somehow historically important for him to document his failure with hard-copy proof.

As he shook his head in amazement at the numerous ways people could say no, he stuffed all the rejections into a green trash bag. It felt good, as if he was saying good-bye to a case of hemorrhoids.

When the phone rang a second time, he saw it was Syd. "Hi, honey," he said.

"I miss you."

"Miss you too.

"When are you coming down here?"

"Next week. Apartment has been cleaned, and I sold most of the furniture. I'll box up all our personal stuff and it will be picked up in a couple days, should be there by Friday."

"Any word from anybody?"

"Just 'nos' and more 'nos.'"

"Unbelievable. A story like that and no one will take it."

"Maybe that's the problem, it's too unbelievable. I probably should have written it as fiction."

"Hey, that's a great idea, why don't you…"

"No, not a chance."

"But…"

"I mean it, not a chance. It's time to find a real job and make some real cash."

"I'll never vote again," Syd said glumly.

"I do have another meeting in a couple days that I might as well go to while I'm still in town. Last-minute thing with Pegasus. Only agency that gave me even a "maybe."

"David, aren't they kind of schlocky? I mean all those conspiracy things they publish."

"I'd take schlocky at this point, but from the looks of them I may have to give *them* an advance."

"How about your agent?"

"She fired me a few months ago. Didn't want to tell you."

"Fuck her."

"Thanks, but no thanks."

"I'm horny, David."

"Can you hold it for another week?"

"I don't know, the Orkin guy was spraying for bugs today and he was looking pretty hot."

"How old?"

"About eighty."

"Okay, but don't hurt him."

"I think he tries to tempt me with that spray wand of his."

"Can't wait to see you." David said.

"A week sounds like such a long time."

"I know. Tell your parents I said 'hi.' I'll call you after the meeting with Pegasus."

"Good luck and don't worry, your story will eventually get out to the world."

When David hung up the phone, he was tempted to call Syd back just. Just because. Instead, he tossed more rejection letters into the green trash bag. The bag was getting full.

CHAPTER 44

BY 4:10 THE NEXT DAY while he sat in a booth at Friday's in Penn Station, David thought he had been stood up by Detective Casey. "Christ, even homicide cops don't want to see me," he had whispered to himself as he sat near the front door of the restaurant. At 4:14 the detective entered, saw David, and waved before making his way over to the table. He wore a topcoat, scarf, skull cap, and gloves.

"Hi, David, I'm Detective Robert Casey, Washington DC Homicide." Casey flipped open his identification, which David scanned. "Thanks for seeing me. Sorry I'm late, I had to go outside and meet Detective Simmons from NYPD and return some of the information he had sent me. We got our butts rained on. By the way, the detective said to say hello to you and Sydney." David rose from the booth and shook Casey's gloved hand.

David also immediately thought to himself that he might now be in trouble with Ernie Simmons since he assumed Casey would have told him that David did indeed at one time, at least, have James' files that had been left in the back of the cab. A fact David had withheld from Ernie. "I sure remember Ernie, he's a good guy. Glad to meet you, but I'm not sure I'll be able to add anything to what you already know."

"You never know. This won't take long. I want to get back to DC before the snow hits. Want something to eat or drink, it's on me?" Casey asked.

"Burger sounds good."

After the food came, the men engaged in some small talk about the Jets and Redskins between bites of cheeseburgers, then Casey got down to business.

"Mind if I take some notes?"

"You cops sure like taking your notes."

"Creatures of habit. Had you ever seen Dr. McDowell before the day you drove him to DC?"

"No. I picked him up in Harlem outside a place called Judi's."

"He must have wanted to get there in a big way. Did he say why he wanted to take a cab rather than take a train?"

"No, he slept most of the way."

"Did he mention anyone following him?"

"No."

"You said it was an Audi that hit him, is that right?"

"I think so, but it could have been a Mercedes or big Lexus, I guess."

"You originally said Audi."

"Did I? It could have been an Audi."

As Casey reviewed his notebook, David yawned. "Sorry, I didn't sleep much last night."

"No problem. When you called Dr. McDowell's room the night he was murdered and spoke to me, you said you had found a briefcase in the back of the cab."

"That's right, it was wedged under the passenger front seat."

"What was in the briefcase?"

"A couple blank yellow tablets, a crossword puzzle book, some pens, a calculator, some condoms, and a bottle of aspirin."

"Anything else in the back of the cab? Any files, papers, anything like that?"

"No, I cleaned it out when I got back to Gino's like I always did, and there was nothing there except the briefcase."

"No papers, no files?"

"Nothing. Clean as a whistle."

"What did you do with the briefcase once you found it?"

"After I found James' reservation at the Hay-Adams in an outside pocket and took out his cell phone to call you, I put everything back in the briefcase and gave it to Gino. He said he was going to take care of it."

"Did he ever tell you what he did with it?"

"No, I never spoke to him again after I gave him the briefcase. He and Marie were murdered that night. Didn't the New York cops find the briefcase?"

"No. They said they found nothing in their house or in the garage. Any idea where Gino may have hidden the briefcase?"

"Why would he hide it? He didn't know it was all that important. People leave things in the back of cabs all the time and call us to get their stuff back or just forget about it. I don't think he would have hidden it."

"Then I wonder what happened to it?" Casey asked.

"Don't have a clue." David said with a shrug.

David yawned again, and his vision began to get fuzzy. He had a hard time understanding Casey's questions. Casey saw David's distress, and after he paid the bill he said. "Hey, it's hot in here. Maybe we should go outside in the cold air to clear your head."

David nodded and with Casey's help got up from the booth and made it to the escalator that would take them outside the station. Casey held onto David's elbow as they finally made their way up into the brisk night air.

At the top of the escalator they turned right at a cab stand onto 8th Avenue. Seconds later a dark Ford Sedan pulled up, and Casey ushered a barely standing David into the back seat and then moved into the seat next to David, then motioned for the driver to go.

In the back of the car, David leaned his head back. "I'm really tired."

"It's from the gloves. Something was also added to your cheeseburger. Stuff is powerful."

"Are you...are you one of them?"

"Afraid so. They are very thorough and very convincing. And, you know, everyone has a price."

As Casey spoke, David had a hard time focusing. His mouth and tongue felt thick. The detective became a blur. Right before he passed out, David gathered his strength for one last statement. "I found...the briefcase...I wrote a book...it's all safe...I know the truth..." David then lapsed into unconsciousness.

CHAPTER 45

Midtown Manhattan Office Tower, March 2013

DAVID CAME OUT OF HIS stupor slowly, like he was rising from the ocean depths to a surface bathed in sunlight. At first he heard only indistinct sounds, not voices exactly, more like low murmurs, almost a monotone hum. Then he thought he heard a man's voice, then two men talking. Then there was another voice, a woman's.

He remembered meeting Casey at Friday's, the cheeseburger, all those questions. So many questions. He remembered getting tired. Going up the escalator, cool air. There was a car. The back seat smelled funny. A cigar? He heard a man's voice say "…everyone has a price."

Then as if a switch had been flipped on, everything came back to David in crystal- clear clarity. Yet even after he had gotten his mental bearings and realized he wasn't dead yet, he kept his eyes closed, hoping the sounds of the voices around him would give him a clue as to where he was and what he would be facing. In the background, he clearly heard a male voice say, "Do you think it was wise to bring him here, Connie?"

A female voice responded, "We need to know everything."

Another male voice said, "He confirmed he found the briefcase and said he wrote a book. Do you believe him?"

The female voice replied, "If he did, he will tell us."

David tried to move his hands, but they were tied behind his back. So were his ankles. He kept his eyes closed when he heard footsteps coming toward him. He was suddenly doused with a pitcher full of ice-cold water. David choked and spat out the water as he gasped for breath.

His eyes opened, but everything around him was a blur. When his surroundings began to at last come into focus, he saw he was in a huge office suite. He was lying on a black leather couch and could see a large chrome and glass desk off to his right. He saw several tall chrome lamps scattered around the suite and off-white carpeting. Outside the floor-to-ceiling windows, he could see the lights of Manhattan and deep into the desolate New Jersey suburban wilderness.

Three impeccably dressed men and a beautiful red-haired woman stood around David with drinks in their hands. In the corner, Detective Robert Casey, one of DC's finest, sat on an overstuffed black chair and casually paged through a newspaper. His pistol was on the table to his right. David looked up at Connie and said simply, "I wrote a book."

Connie stood over David and casually stirred her drink with a chrome swizzle stick. She was dressed in a cream-colored custom-made, two-thousand-dollar St. John's knit suit, Stuart Weitzman alligator skin pumps, and a diamond brooch from Tiffany's. "How utterly and completely exciting for you, David."

"My book tells all about what you guys have been doing for over sixty years. All of it."

"Oh my, David, you must have agents, editors, publishers and even movie studios beating a path to your door, breathless in anticipation. I'm sure they are ready to write huge advance checks to get their hands on such an amazing, albeit difficult to believe, story."

"Oh yeah. They're going nuts for my story. It's gonna be a best seller."

"So all those copies of rejection letters in your trash, some as a recent as yesterday, were just the ones who said no?"

"Well, I admit, it's not for everybody."

"Obviously. The question is, is it for anybody?"

"Sure, tons of interest. I even was told they might make a movie out of it."

"Really? I wonder whom would play me?" Connie asked.

"You know, after I saw a bunch of those photo-shopped pictures on the net with you all dolled up in those fancy dresses, I would have suggested maybe Diane Lane or Julianne Moore."

"How very flattering of you. They are two of my favorite actresses."

Yeah, but now that I have seen you in person, I think I'm going to suggest Danny DeVito instead." The men in dark expensive suits snickered at David's remark. Connie glared at the men, who suddenly regained stern looks on their faces and in turn glared at David.

"David, for someone who may find himself tossed off this building in three minutes, you are awfully snide. Even rude."

"Yeah, I tend to get that way when I'm lied to, drugged, hog-tied, and have water thrown in my face."

"You know, David, everything that has happened over the last several months could have been avoided if you had just done the right thing and returned our briefcase."

"Yeah, I'm sure you would have given me a reward for all those files and just let me go."

"We'll never know, will we?"

"I have a pretty good idea. Look, I sent a half dozen flash drives with my story and copies of the files to my attorney, my agent, and four friends with instructions to send them to the *Washington Post* and *New York Times* in case I died, no matter how I died. So even if I don't get my story published, which I sure as hell will, your ass will still be in a sling when people read what I wrote."

"How so? You didn't know who I was when you wrote your little book, and you don't really even know who I am now. And you have absolutely no proof of anything except for some stolen files taken by a terminated, disgruntled ex-employee, who undoubtedly corrupted and/or altered those files before he got himself robbed and killed in a DC hotel. Hardly a rare or newsworthy occurrence."

"Connie, if you're so sure of yourself, why haven't you killed me already?" David asked, not sure he wanted to hear her answer.

"Curiosity."

"Look, I have a deal for you. Kind of a win-win. You give me a million dollars cash, and I'll pull my story and write something else. A self-help book of some kind. Or maybe a vampire trilogy dedicated to the youth of America."

"Give me some time to ponder your generous proposal. But, no matter what, David, I must admit, you have done a fine investigative job. Really quite well done. You are indeed a fine writer."

"You tend to do your homework when people try to kill you and yours."

"I can appreciate that."

"Wait a minute," David said, as the fog continued to lift from his brain. "How do you know what I wrote?"

"David, you have been shopping your manuscript all over town for weeks now. We have friends in many corners of this city, people who protect us, and keep us informed if someone or something puts us at risk. And I must say, your book, although unbelievable on many levels, could cause us some discomfort."

"First of all, you haven't seen everything. Since I sent my original manuscript a few weeks ago, which you apparently got your hands on, I have done a complete rewrite and in it, I specifically name you and all the lap dogs who work for you by name, including Mr. Flagel standing over there. Earlier this week, I sent that rewrite to a couple dozen agents, editors, and publishers."

The very well-dressed Stephan Flagel suddenly got a "who me?" look on his face and almost swallowed both olives in his martini.

"Given our rather extensive contacts around the city, I think I would have seen your final product by now, David, if you had indeed done as you say."

"I doubt even you know every publisher, editor, and agent in New York, Connie. And even fewer in DC, Chicago, and L.A."

Connie smiled at David and said, "Not all."

"You mentioned discomfort, Connie. By the looks of you and this office, you don't appear to be the kind of woman who enjoys discomfort of any kind." David said.

"That is very perceptive on your part, David. It's true I do make a habit of avoiding or eliminating things or people that create problems for me and my associates."

"Well then, Connie, it sounds like we have the makings of a mutually beneficial deal. One that works for both of us. I give you my book, and you give me your cash. Sounds fair to me."

"If I could somehow be assured, I have all copies of your manuscript then perhaps…"

"Please, Connie. That would be really stupid on my part, wouldn't it? I give you all my work, and I end up very dead anyway. That sounds like a real bad deal for me. Besides, you could always come after me and my family later if I did release my book at some point in the future."

"That would be revenge, not prevention. And I am very much into prevention. But I must admit yours is an offer to consider. However, I think we might be able to convince you to pull your story without the need for cash or worse, my group living under the cloud of you someday changing your mind and releasing your book. For instance, we could make *you* an offer."

"I'm listening."

"If you agree to pull your book and provide us absolute assurances we have all copies, we will promise not to give you a DVD of your beautiful wife and her parents being sliced up with machetes by some Haitian friends of ours down in Boca Raton."

David did not flinch or hesitate. "Keep it up, bitch, and the price goes to two million."

Connie's face grew hard even though she forced a tight smile. "David, I admire someone trying to gamble with no chips, but I fear you are out of your league in terms of negotiation skills."

"Maybe you're right, Connie. But I do know whatever you'd pay me is chump change compared to the damage my book could do to you in terms of congressional inquiries, Senate subcommittee hearings, attorney fees, and cable TV making millions of people in this country and around the world, wondering if this entire government and democracy, as a form of government, is a total and unadulterated fraud."

"To prove such an incredible and unlikely story, you will need unassailable proof, and all you have are a few easily explained files and memos. Hardly the kind of information that could cause us meaningful problems."

"You say I don't know who you are, but I do. You are Constance Suzanne Reynolds. Granddaughter of William Baker Reynolds, who started your company in 1948. All this crap began when Truman surprisingly beat Dewey that year. That screwed up everybody in this country and around the world, since the big money had already bet on Dewey. That happened because the polls were wrong."

"Really? Please go on." Connie said with a smile.

"Your grandfather met with some other rich guys, and they came up with a plan to never let that happen again. So, it started with Eisenhower versus Stevenson in 1952. Since that time there have been no surprises. Surprises can be painful. And expensive. Very expensive."

Connie stared at David for several moments. The men in suits looked at each other with concern. "Indeed, it appears you are an excellent investigative reporter, David." Connie turned and spoke to the men around her, "Gentlemen, would you please leave the room and let David and me have a few words in private?"

CHAPTER 46

AFTER THE FOUR MEN, INCLUDING the detective, left the room, Connie refreshed her drink, then moved to a comfortable chair near the couch where David was still tied up. She sat down and stared at David silently for several moments, as if trying to size up the man she felt was trying to destroy her company and her country.

Finally, David asked, "Don't guess you'd consider untying me while we talk, would you?"

"Not hardly. Especially not after what I heard you did to a couple friends of mine recently. That was very impressive."

"Thanks. But I think your selection process for friends needs a little work."

"Perhaps, but in the scheme of things, everyone serves a purpose." Connie said as she sipped her Manhattan.

"What now?"

"What now is that you are regrettably but most assuredly going to die, David. The only questions remaining are how you will die and if you want to see your wife and her parents also die because of your lack of cooperation."

"What kind of cooperation do you have in mind?"

"I want you to turn all your work over to us including physical copies, hard drives, flash drives, notes, files, everything and anything associated with your book. In exchange, you have my word your wife and her family will remain safe."

"Let me think about it. But for now, will you be kind enough to answer some questions for me first? I mean if I am going to die anyway... you know, I am an inquisitive investigative writer."

"Of course, I completely understand, please, ask away, David." Connie said with a smile.

"How in the hell have you managed to keep what you do secret for so long?"

"You were right; it began with my grandfather after the election in 1948. The whole world thought Dewey was going to win the election. The fact was he *should* have won the election. He was without question the far stronger candidate and would have proven to be a far stronger leader domestically and around the world. He was an educated, articulate, and proven entity. He had been tested and had proved his mettle over several decades. Truman, on the other hand, was a crude clown. He had neither the temperament nor the intellect to serve as our president."

"He was smart enough to get elected."

"Truman, among many others before him, proved any fool can get elected. Just tell the rabble what they want to hear, say the country is in peril from outsiders, make promises that will never be kept, talk in short sentences repeating the same pabulum no matter how idiotic, and the low IQ voters in this country will elect such a person."

"Doesn't the Constitution give the voters that right?"

"No, it specifically does not guarantee a vote for any person, it only says people cannot be stopped from voting based on certain criteria. But it also says it is treason not to defend this country from enemies 'foreign and domestic,' and that is what my group has always done. We have defended this country from a potential electorate that has not as yet earned the guarantee you say is in the Constitution."

"That's a rather broad interpretation of that line about defending the country and I'm not even sure it's in the Constitution either." David said.

"My grandfather believed in any interpretation of any document that protected this country. He and many other brilliant people felt Truman was a huge mistake and an even bigger risk. But at the time, so did the polls. It was a *sure thing* according to those polls. Dewey couldn't lose.

"So how did he lose?"

"He made the unfortunate assumption that he was talking to educated, informed people on the campaign trail. His rhetoric was way over their heads. He never connected with the people."

"So Truman just ran a smarter campaign?"

"Insofar as dumbing down his speeches, yes, but that was based on a political calculation, not one based on policy, or even a respect for the voter. He knew they were stupid and ignorant, and he played to that stupidity and ignorance."

"Sounds pretty smart to me."

"Perhaps. But based on the assumption Dewey was going to win, hundreds of millions of dollars were spent in preparation to put the right people in the right places, pay off politicians to vote a certain way, work with labor unions, banks, even foreign governments. Then all that money was lost when Truman won. Further, Truman was a buffoon, with all that 'Give 'em hell' nonsense. He had no right nor the qualifications to run this country."

"Except that the American people voted for him, and Truman wasn't all bad. He started NATO, the Marshall Plan, the Truman Doctrine…" David interjected.

"Please David, have a sense of history. Have you forgotten

the dropping of the atomic bombs? The Korean War? The hundreds of thousands of people killed? Our group had already negotiated a peace treaty with Japan before Roosevelt died. Dewey would have ended the war with no atomic bomb. Further, until Truman interfered, we had North Korea prepared to accept a co-existence agreement to avoid a war and eliminate that 38th Parallel foolishness that is still haunting us today. He was an abomination and embarrassment to this country. But he did teach us a painful lesson and my organization vowed such a thing would never happen again."

"How could you have been so sure how presidents would have reacted once they were in office?"

"Because they had been vetted and we *knew* how they would react to certain circumstances. However, if we felt there was a chance they would move in a direction we did not agree with, we were prepared to use our financial resources to dispense whatever statistical information needed to the public that would sell any policy, including even a declaration of war. And if need be, we were prepared to spend whatever cash needed to be spent to ensure an appropriate policy was put in place."

"What about the House and Senate, they could override a president on any issue, it happens all the time." David declared.

"No, it doesn't. We have found the men and women in Congress are even easier to push toward an issue. Again, all it takes is money, and we have plenty of money." Connie explained.

"So you just ignore the Constitution and the voting public?"

"Do you really think the uneducated and uninformed voters of this country know who is best suited to become the most powerful person in the world? Please, the stupidity within the electorate of this country is mind numbing. Plus more than half of the American people don't even vote, which is a higher non-voting percentage than any other democracy in the world."

Connie rose from her chair and began to walk around her office with her drink in her hand as she continued her American civics lesson. "The majority of the half of the population that does vote can be lured by any charlatan who promises them a newer car or an extra week's vacation at Disney World. Americans don't deserve a say in who runs this country. They forfeited that right long ago."

"So you really think you and your group are providing a public service to this country by, in essence, selecting the president every four years?"

"We are without question providing stability both domestically and internationally. We also provide controlled leadership that has been evaluated by the most brilliant minds in this country. As a result, financial markets remain calm; people can go about their everyday lives without worrying about someone gaining access to the White House that could cause domestic and international chaos. Even world wars. We care less about the petty domestic squabbles like abortion, health care, or even racial issues, and allow the politicians to handle that kind of minutia. All we are concerned about is ensuring this country does not go off the rails because of a president who is unprepared, incompetent, or even mentally ill."

"Do you really believe the citizens of this country could be duped by someone so uniquely unqualified as to, in essence, ruin this country in four or even eight years after we have survived forty-four presidents over two and a half centuries?"

"Dear God yes, David, a thousand times yes. Without our processes and people in place, this country is capable of electing anyone who promises them what they want to hear. All it would take is the mere perception that things are worse than they really are. Or someone to say we are in danger, or state we are at risk from a foreign entity in some undisclosed or fabricated way like Joe McCarthy did. Those lies coupled with a smooth-talking deliverer of a bad message, and the American public would leap at the chance to put someone in charge who could undo two hundred and fifty years of this country's heritage."

"Isn't that exactly what you are doing? You are undermining the Constitution by what you do. Can't you see that?"

"Over the last sixty-plus years, our group has managed this country in its best interests. We have been fair to both parties, and the results speak for themselves. Under our guidance, America has emerged as the only superpower in the world, defeated communism, created an unbeatable military, the world's strongest economy, relative social and political stability, plus we are respected and feared around the world. Americans have never had more freedom, wealth, or opportunity. I would give us a solid A for our efforts."

"What gives you the right to unilaterally make those decisions?"

"We simply love our country more than you and the rest of the population does. We also see its glorious potential. That gives us the absolute right to make those decisions. But more importantly, we are willing and able to make the tough decisions as well when we have to."

"Like what?"

"Like when a handsome young president can't keep his dick in his pants and was about to be blackmailed by both the Mafia and the Russian government because of information they had uncovered on him. As a result, we did what needed to be done."

"That's bullshit, you guys didn't..."

"My grandfather's aggressive and patriotic action saved our country a decade of investigations, a falling stock market, maybe even a depression, or worse, an utter and complete financial meltdown."

"You mean a United States president was assassinated over money?"

"That was certainly a major part of it, but there would also have been international instability, perhaps the spread of communism, and domestically things like civil rights and the space program would never have made it through Congress with a politically wounded president."

"So your group just murdered...?"

"Grandfather did what had to be done. And it was incredibly easy to find the fools to carry out the task. The same with Nixon, it was a hard choice but the right one. If it wasn't for Deep Throat who was on our payroll, the public would have let Tricky Dick slide and crippling political unrest would have resulted. We have always acted in the long-term best interests of this country as an institution and protected the American people."

"How did you respond to the unforeseen? Like 9/11?"

"That event was only unforeseen by political leaders not paying attention. We saw it coming years in advance. That's why we needed Cheney in place to ensure that when it happened, there would be at least a financial advantage to those of our friends who months before invested millions into companies that would provide munitions and equipment for the resulting and inevitable war effort."

"You mean you let 9/11 happen so people on your team could make a fucking profit?"

"Eighteen months before the event, we knew it was going to happen in some form in some major American city. So if it was inevitable, why not put an administration in place that would react the way we wanted it to react?"

"Did you ever think of contacting your local congressman?"

"I think even you understand the folly in such an effort," Connie said with a smile.

"Okay, you got me there."

"We feared Gore would have been too weak to respond forcefully to the attack we had learned was absolutely going to take place. We knew Bush could be led by the rest of the hawks and create billions of profits for those who supported our efforts," Connie explained logically.

"You mean by invading a country that had nothing to do with 9/11?"

"There are times when profit taking is required and acceptable. Invading Afghanistan and Iraq and the resulting need for military armaments allowed us to repay favors and provide a return on investment for all involved in our enterprise."

"Why are you telling me all this? Looking for a way to confess your sins?"

"David, you are so smug in your certitude. You think you have *right* on your side so that makes what we do so abhorrent in your eyes. Who are the real patriots here? People like you who write books that could destroy the country? Or the fools who would vote in an idiot president on the pledge of a new dishwasher?"

"It's called a democracy for a reason..."

"Your naïveté is stunning," Connie said.

"Your so-called patriotism is laughable."

"We believe the real patriots in this country are those of us who see the true greatness in this country, who want it to survive and flourish for a thousand years, and be the undisputed world leader during that time. We protect this country while people like you try to undermine it, even destroy it."

"You mean you protect it as long as there is a profit in doing so."

"Don't be so idealistic and sanctimonious. Didn't you write your book to make money?"

David ignored Connie's question and asked his own. "Sounds like murder is also an option you partake of on a regular basis."

"*Elimination* of a problem or potential problem, like you, is in fact a viable tool at times. I won't deny that. But in comparison to what damage a single person or small group can heap upon this nation, and even the rest of the world, such actions are more than justified; they are in fact a duty and responsibility of those of us who truly love America."

"It seems in reality that you have little faith in this country or our people. You think they need *you* to find the right path. I don't. I think people will, in the end, make the right choices and the right decisions. They may not always get it right, but they will figure it out in the end."

"At what cost, David? You are willing to risk this nation's future on an electorate that just doesn't care and is too stupid to learn. They are too busy on Twitter, or YouTube, or their smartphones to care about this nation. Those people have, with their ignorance, stupidity, and laziness abdicated their responsibility to us."

"You say you care? You care so much you tear down the Constitution to get what you want?"

"It's not what we want; it's what this country must have." Connie said.

"Talk about being smug."

"Even the half of this country that does vote does so as part of a herd mentality based on a ridiculous two-party system with no real thought behind what is best for America, only what is best for their party. Yet, that foolishness inures to our benefit and is why it is so easy to sway them with numbers. Numbers don't require thought; they are the shorthand for the idiot class. We also learned over time the fewer the numbers the better, less confusion for the masses."

"Is that why after all the polling, all the other superfluous statistical bullshit, unemployment rates were the ones you focused on and what drove the voters?"

"Very good, David. 'Keep it simple, stupid' does work with a voting class that can be bought with a dollar an hour increase in their paycheck or the promise of a job that will never come to fruition. There are times we will get involved with other lesser issues as circumstances dictate, but unemployment is the key issue on so many levels. Maybe someday your fantasy America will exist, but it doesn't exist today. And until it does, my group and I will protect it while you write books that can destroy it."

"You are certifiably fucked up."

"Fortunately, not everyone thinks so. David, you need to decide relative to your wife and her family and the work you've done. What will it be?"

"There is no decision. Based on what you just said, my wife, her parents, and I are all dead either way. You couldn't possibly take a chance and let any of us live."

Returning to her seat near David, Connie stared at him for several moments then asked, "What if you did expose us to the world and bring us down? What then? Don't you realize that if my group doesn't protect this country by putting the right people in place, other nations or even far-right factions including neo-Nazis already in this country will step into the breech and take over our elections?"

"You're crazy."

"No, I'm not. The technology is already there to do exactly what I said. It's possible that a foreign entity could gain control of our election process. And don't underestimate what groups already in this country could do in terms of breeching our voting systems that could lead them to put in place a friendly far right wing or left wing administration that could undermine everything this country has stood for the last two hundred and fifty years. Even a one-term president is capable of doing incalculable damage."

"If our country can defeat Hitler, Mussolini, Japan, overcome polio, smog, the Edsel, Duck Dynasty, and Honey Boo Boo, I think we could handle some third-rate power from impacting our elections. Hell, isn't that exactly what you're doing?"

"My God, you're pathetic. You see yourself as a soldier for truth, justice, and the American Way. Can't you see that if a foreign entity or white nationalist group impacted our elections that is the least damage they could do? The real damage would be whom they would put in place to run this country. Our approach is not and has never been to just arbitrarily sway the vote. It is to protect our country by whom we put in place as president. Someone that will protect and elevate this country, not destroy it."

"Our country will not be destroyed by a single bad president, no matter who it is. It could face some tough times, but if that were to be the case, I want to at least bring you and your cabal down for what you have done," David said.

"How stupidly gallant. Here's the flaw in your argument, David. If another country were to replace us in selecting a president, say China, Russia, North Korea, or maybe even a well-disguised far right or far left internal group, and given the means and opportunity they most certainly would, you would not even know that it occurred until it was too late. Perhaps thirty years from now, everything you say you love about this country today would be gone. All gone and replaced by a country you will not recognize. A country controlled by an outside, unseen power. Piece by piece, your freedoms, your rights, your way of life, our country's reputation, prestige, financial, and military position in the world would be gone, and you would not even know it had happened."

For several moments Connie and David stared at each other, and both realized there was nothing more to say.

Connie pushed a button on her table, and the three men in suits along with the detective came back into the room. Connie looked at Detective Casey and motioned him over to the couch. "Detective, David and I have concluded our conversation. I believe he is lying about having sent that information to other sources. He does not strike me as someone who would be that careful or strategic. Please dispose of David while we are at dinner in a manner consistent with someone who has tried to extort me and who is intent on undermining this country by his traitorous actions."

Casey nodded. Connie and the three men in suits walked toward the front door of the office.

Connie stopped at the door and had parting words for David. "David, seconds before your pending demise, I hope you envision what awaits your wife and her family given their knowledge of our enterprise. I only regret you have no children we could add to your final thoughts."

"Hey Connie, my final offer is three million, and Jon Voight playing you in the movie."

Casey raised his pistol and smashed it into the side of David's head, knocking him out.

CHAPTER 47

DAVID AWOKE IN DARKNESS WITH his arms and legs still tied. He felt motion and quickly realized he was in the trunk of a moving car. He remembered his cell phone, but it was no longer in his pocket and he couldn't have reached it if it was. With a head that ached, he tried to think while being jostled along a high-speed road.

From the sounds coming from the outside, David surmised that the car was going at least sixty miles an hour, which meant he was no longer in Manhattan. He had no idea how long he had been unconscious, but his shirt was still wet from the water Connie had thrown on him, so he reasoned it could not have been that long.

He lay on his left side with his hands still tied behind his back, the plastic ties rubbing his skin raw and creating deep red crevices around his wrists. His ankles were also still tied, and the restraints had cut off the blood supply causing his feet to become cold and numb.

He felt along the floor of the interior of the trunk for something, most notably a safety latch that would have opened the trunk. Either it had been removed or he just couldn't find it. All he could feel was a rubber mat. Using his feet, he scrunched up the mat and used his bound hands and fingers to again investigate in the darkness.

His fingers felt for something, for anything, but the spare tire under the floor mat was not the solution he had hoped for. But then after a few more minutes, he realized he had found something that might be what he was looking for. It was the tire jack assembly in the center of the spare tire, if he could only remember how the hell those things worked and exactly what it was he was touching in the darkness.

He continued his behind-the-back in-the-dark search until he found the lug nut wrench. He tried to pull the wrench free, but it wouldn't budge. He then vaguely remembered that the last time he had changed a tire, he had to unscrew something. With that sliver of memory as a guidepost, David began to twist each metal part in the middle of the tire. He had to stop and tried to recall if it was "lefty loosey, righty tighty." It was.

Once he had freed the wrench, and knowing his legs were four times stronger than his arms, he turned over on his back and used his bound feet to try to pick it up. After several frustrating attempts he finally secured the wrench between his feet and began to pound it against the rear taillight assembly, hoping he could break it out and get someone's attention on the road.

The problem was he was already getting the attention of Detective

Casey, who had decided it might be best for him to take the next exit off the Long Island Expressway and see what was happening with his boisterous passenger in the Ford's trunk.

When he failed to break the taillight from the inside, David stabbed at the lock a dozen times hoping to break it, but he couldn't find the right spot. After that maneuver failed, he turned on his side and tried to place the flat end of the wrench in the metal seam of the trunk lid with his hands. After at least twenty jabs, he felt the wrench stick in the seam right inside the rubber molding that lined the trunk.

As he felt the car turn and begin to slow on the ramp Casey had taken, David pushed down as hard as he could on the wrench. With a last thrust, the trunk lid burst open. As the Ford continued to slow, the trunk lid began to bounce up and down off the wrench David had left under the trunk lid. He could see a car following the Ford off the exit ramp, and he had a tough decision to make. Either stay in the trunk and *sure as hell* get killed by Casey or roll out of the Ford and *probably* get killed by whatever was following it.

Before he took the latter of the two not so good options, he said to himself, "Well, this is going to leave a mark." It did.

The initial impact of David hitting the exit ramp was surprisingly painless. It was the uncontrolled rolling caused by exiting a Ford moving at thirty-five miles per hour that caused the second, third and fourth bounces to be far more painful, especially when he left a significant amount of skin from his face on the pavement.

When he finally stopped rolling, he came face-to-face with a Mercedes 560SL. The gray-haired elderly woman who drove the Benz was barely visible above the steering wheel, but her quick reflexes belied her age. As soon as she saw David explode from the back of the Ford, she hit the brakes and was able to stop the pride of German engineering three inches from David's skull.

Further down the ramp, Casey had seen in his side view mirror what had happened and quickly pulled off to the side of the road. With pistol in hand, Casey ran back to where David had landed and to where he was now being tended to by the elderly woman. "Oh, my God! Young man, are you hurt?" she asked.

Before David could answer in the affirmative, that yes he was sure as hell hurt, Casey arrived on the scene. "Lady, I'm a police officer, and this man is under arrest. Get back in your car and move on."

"But this boy is injured, and why would a police officer keep someone under arrest tied up in a trunk?"

Casey pulled his Washington DC police ID from his pocket, flipped it open, and showed it to the smallish octogenarian.

"Lady, I don't have time to fool with you Get back in your car and get out of here now, or I'll have to arrest you too. I mean it"

The small old woman wore an expensive blue blazer, with cream-colored slacks, and a white silk blouse accented with a double strand of genuine cultured pearls. Her expensive blue suede shoes had a crest on the toes.

She did not appear to be the least bit intimidated by Casey's demand to leave the scene and instead took her time when she looked closely at his ID. Then she looked even more closely at David. But then she simply shrugged her shoulders, shook her head, mumbled something under her breath, and walked toward her Benz.

After the woman left, Casey returned his gun to its holster, reached down and pulled David back to his feet. He lifted him over his shoulder in a perfect execution of the "fireman's carry" and lugged him back to the Ford.

After he opened the rear door and was prepared to throw David into the back seat, he felt the barrel of a Glock .357 Sig at the base of his spine being held by the well-dressed gray-haired Mercedes aficionado, who was now packing heat.

"My husband was a judge around here for thirty years and I know this is not your jurisdiction even if you really are a DC cop. Hell, you could be a local drug dealer for all I know. So let's call the Long Island Police and see what's going on here."

Looking over his shoulder, Casey said, "Lady, don't make me hurt..."

"Don't you mess with me, pal. I've already shot a mugger in the city and some punk trying to break into my beach house. I'll put a bullet in your ass sure as hell if you try anything with me. Now put your hands on the top of that car and stay put. I mean it. Don't get me mad now."

Casey believed her about shooting those guys and put his hands on the roof of the Ford. The woman reached into Casey's pocket, pulled out his pistol, and tossed it into the bushes behind her.

David was still standing next to the Ford, balanced on two legs that remained tied at the ankles. "Thank you, ma'am. He was going to kill me. I doubt I would have ever gotten out of that car alive."

"Don't thank me yet, young man. I'm calling the local police right now." The woman dialed the police on her cell and, after some pleasantries with the officer on the phone, gave him her location and told him he may want to send some backup.

After her call, the woman turned to David and asked, "Why was this man going to kill you, young man?"

"It's kind of a long story, ma'am. But I am very grateful you called the police."

"Was he going to kill you because you needed killing? What if you are murderer or rapist or a Mafia guy?"

"No ma'am, actually, I'm just a writer. And I wrote a book that can get this guy, his boss, and a bunch of other folks, really bad folks, in a lot of trouble."

"A writer? How nice. My grandson is a writer, but he writes cooking articles for a paper in San Francisco."

"Ma'am, this guy is a real cop, but he's a real bad one. He and his friends have already murdered three people and tried killing my wife and me in order to get me to stop writing my book."

"Well, let's just wait for the police to come, and we'll settle all this."

"I'm fine with that. But I doubt he'll be." David said.

Looking toward Casey, the woman asked, "Hey mister, are you okay with the police coming?"

"Sure, why not? But you're the one that should be worried since you are obstructing justice. You'll probably get arrested and put in jail."

"Oh, I'm not worried. I know all these kids on the force through my husband, who was a local judge around here for thirty years. We've donated millions to the Long Island FOP over the years. They're all good boys."

After his bluff did not work, Casey quickly and unwisely decided on another plan. He suddenly turned and drove his shoulder into the old woman, knocking her to the ground, and ran across the ramp towards the woods.

Unfortunately, his peripheral vision, foot speed, and general quickness were not what they once were. As a result of those declining physical skills, an eighteen-wheel Peterbilt semi, rolling down the ramp hauling tons of rolled steel, had just enough time for a single horn blast before it virtually liquefied Casey when nine of its wheels ran over him from head to toe.

When the old woman picked herself up off the ground and looked onto the ramp and saw what a mess Casey had made of himself, she said, "Well, it certainly looks like *someone* had something to hide. Innocent people don't run away like that. That's what my late husband Merle used to say, and he was a wonderful man."

When the apoplectic truck driver who had pulled over and parked his truck on the shoulder ran back to see what was left of Casey, he began to wail, "Oh God, is he dead? Oh, God, is he dead?"

"Is he dead?" asked the old woman calmly. "For heaven's sake, young man, he looks like a crushed grape. I'd say he's very, very dead. But don't worry, he ran out in front of you. I'll tell the cops, and you can be on your way in no time. Just go have a seat in your truck and try to calm down, son."

After the young driver finally composed himself and obeyed the old woman, she put her Glock back into her purse and pulled out another pistol while she searched for her Swiss Army knife and cell phone. She turned to David and asked, "If I cut you loose, will you promise not to run away before the cops get here?"

"I promise not to run away, but I wish you would let me go so I can get back to the city. My wife and her family are in danger, and I have to contact her as soon as I can. If I don't, this guy's friends will kill them."

"What's the name of your book?"

"STATS"…like in statistics."

"What's it about?"

"How all the statistics we hear on radio and TV and see in the papers are made up to make us vote a certain way."

"Is that really news? I mean who believes that stuff anyway?"

"A lot of people do."

"I guess."

"How will you get back to the city?"

"I could hitch…"

"Don't be silly. If you walk a mile up this road, there's a train station down on the left. You can catch the train or grab a cab there. Do you have any cash?"

David checked and found his wallet, but the cash was gone. "No."

The old woman put her cell down, reached into her purse, and pulled out two one hundred dollar bills. "Here, take this and go save your wife, her family, and our democracy."

"What's your name?" David asked.

"Millie Hough, pronounced h-o-w. By the way, you might need this. Millie handed David the .38 from her purse. "It's loaded so be careful. Ever used a gun before?"

"Yes ma'am, I have. I swear I'll pay you back." David said as he kissed Millie on the forehead.

"No need, just send me a copy of your book. I'd let you use my cell to call your family, but the cops will be here soon. You go on now and I'll take care of all this."

After Millie cut off the plastic ties, David turned and began jogging toward the train station. From a pay phone at the station he called Syd. "Just make sure you and your parents stay away from their house until you hear from me."

"After you called the last time, I didn't like what I was hearing, so I made a reservation here at the club for the week."

"Good, that's a relief. I'll stop by Verizon first thing in the morning and get a replacement phone so I can stay in touch."

"Get a new number."

"Good idea, I will."

"And don't go near the apartment." Syd said.

"Okay."

"Will this ever be over?"

"Soon. I love you."

"I love you too."

CHAPTER 48

DAVID STEPPED OFF THE TRAIN later that night looking like a train wreck. His clothes were dirty, his face was awash in scrapes and cuts, and he had a three-day beard. He exited the train station with a noticeable limp, hailed a cab, and went directly where Syd had told him not to go. He didn't want to worry her. After all, given what he had already been through that night, how bad could a visit to his old apartment be?

Before he entered his apartment, David did a kind of stakeout of his own building from across the street. For nearly an hour, he stood in the shadows to determine if anyone else was doing the same thing. He checked to see if any cars, particularly Audis, were driving past. The street was Audi-free.

When he finally felt it was safe, he entered his apartment lit only by an outside streetlamp. He regretted that he had had the power turned off earlier that afternoon. He wondered when the last time a utility company had been that efficient.

On the other hand, he was happy the building super had not already changed the locks, or the door would have had to be broken down a second time. The apartment was empty except for a chair, a small table, a large gym bag, and a Mets cap. He put on the cap.

He moved to the kitchen and pulled the stove from the wall. He quickly gathered several manila files that held James' documents and stuffed them into the gym bag. He shoved the pistol that Millie had given him into his pocket after first checking to see if it was really loaded. It was. He smiled and thought of Syd.

After he pushed the stove back into place, he picked up the gym bag and started toward the front door. Only three feet from the door, he heard someone try the handle. The door slowly opened. David backed away and melted into the darkness of the hallway.

Someone entered the apartment and stood near the doorway for several seconds. David raised the .38. Whoever had entered suddenly backed out of the apartment and shut the door after they had locked it from the inside. David could hear their footsteps as they went down the stairs.

He had not intended to stay in the apartment that night. The plan was to swoop into the unit, grab James' files, and get the hell out as fast as he could. So, just to be safe, he decided he would stay in the hall closet for a few minutes after whoever had visited had left the apartment building. That was when he discovered he was beyond tired, beyond exhausted; it was something near death. Something David had only experienced once before in his life. He knew that kind of exhaustion was dangerous and led to bad decisions and to people getting hurt or even killed.

He told himself he would just take a catnap on the closet floor then get up in time to take a cold shower and make it over to Pegasus before renting a car and driving down to Florida. He drifted off to sleep thinking of Syd. Then it was morning.

CHAPTER 49

DAVID HAD NOT MOVED AN inch all night. When he awoke, his body was stiff and ached from the events of the night before. The fall from the Ford onto the pavement had left a deep, bloody gouge on his right cheekbone. His legs, shoulders, and arms were bruised, and he discovered a goose egg-sized lump on the back of his head. His wrists and ankles were worn raw from the plastic ties that had encircled them for hours.

After taking his early morning pee and finding a significant amount of blood in his urine, caused no doubt by some seriously bruised kidneys, he concluded he didn't have time for even a cold shower. However, he did have time to stop in a Starbucks where he bought two bottles of cranberry juice, two bottles of water, two cans of Red Bull, and two glazed donuts. "Ah, the breakfast of champions," he said to himself.

After his training-room meal, he stopped at the Verizon store and got a replacement phone with a new number. He immediately called Syd and told her some of what had happened the night before. He didn't want to worry her with too much information.

"My God, you are lucky to be alive. I want you to get out of that damn town and get your ass down here ASAP; that's an order, sailor."

David said he would obviously obey her order since she did outrank him and promised he would leave town as soon as his meeting with Pegasus was over.

"Why are you even wasting your time going to that schlock publisher?" she had asked. "Have you seen some of their stuff? All they publish are books about UFOs, Big Foot, and Jesus' image being discovered on a piece of whole wheat toast."

"Yeah, you're probably right. They may be too sophisticated to publish a book about how a group of rich folks have manipulated our votes for almost seventy years, killed Kennedy, installed nine presidents, two vice-presidents, negotiated foreign policy, usurped the Constitution, and murdered people on a regular basis."

After several moments to reflect, Syd said, "Okay, I see your point. But I want your butt out of New York this afternoon." It did in fact sound like an order.

After he said, "Yes ma'am," he gave her his new cell number and told her he would be renting a car and leaving that very afternoon to come to Florida. She agreed that it was a good idea for him not to fly since Connie's friends may be waiting for him at the airport, among many other places.

Later, as David walked through Central Park, he read a headline on a newsfeed on his cell: *A Washington DC detective, Robert Casey, was struck and killed last night when he wandered into the path of a Federal Steel truck just off the Long Island Expressway. Details of the accident are being investigated at this time, including the search for a witness described as a white male in his thirties. He may have suffered injuries at the scene of the accident.*

After reading the account of the untimely demise of Detective Casey, David was tempted to forget about the meeting with Pegasus and immediately leave town. He figured with a few stops for naps along the way, he could make it down to Boca in about eighteen hours and maybe even be able to be in bed with Syd that very night.

Instead, he decided what the hell, he didn't have much to lose by taking the time to call on that loser publisher. Maybe he was their kind of loser.

Later that day David opened the door to Pegasus Publishing and saw eight other losers, including a receptionist named Brianna, in the lobby. He figured he would fit right in with that group.

CHAPTER 50

Pegasus Publishing, Manhattan, March 2013

"SO, THAT'S WHAT HAPPENED. I don't know who came into my apartment last night. It could have been the super or maybe it was one of Connie's boys. Hell, it could have been a neighbor who saw the door ajar. I just don't know. Guess I'm a little paranoid at this point."

The assorted group of writers, agents, job applicants, receptionist, and one editor who had listened to David's tale sat in stunned silence.

"Holy fucking wow, what a story," Walter, the writer of lesbian vampire novels, opined.

"David, did you write the story as fiction or non-fiction?" Jonathan asked.

"Non-fiction. It's all true. Except I didn't have the last 24 hours in it."

"You really need to add that part," said Ricardo, the writer of *The Ultimate Nazi Cookbook.*

"Even if that story isn't true and you made it all up, it's a great story," Cliff, the writer of the puppy/unicorn book, said.

"I didn't make it up, I…"

"I believe your story, David. And even a poor writer could make your story a compelling read. But I doubt any publisher would even touch what you've written," Jonathan said flatly.

"Why the hell not?" Ricardo asked. "It would be a great read."

"It would also be a great lawsuit." Jonathan said. "In fact, it would invite numerous lawsuits for libel, defamation of character, and if you go on radio and TV to market the book, tons of slander claims. The legal fees alone would far outweigh the profits no matter how many books were sold. Plus the publisher would become the *National Enquirer* of book publishing. It's just too hot a subject."

"Isn't that what you guys already are?" Mary, an agent, asked demurely.

"That's true, but we aren't sued by aliens or a dead Elvis," Jonathan Marshall, the editor, said proudly.

"But if David's story is true, and after hearing it, I think it is, this would make Watergate sound like Mary Poppins. Why not take it to the big newspapers and let them run with it?" Muriel, the job seeker, asked.

"I have. I sent it to the *Washington Post, New York Times, LA Times, Chicago Tribune,* and a half dozen other papers and got no response," David explained.

"No wonder you went Rambo earlier. No offense," Walter said.

"None taken," David said glumly.

For several moments there was silence and a decided air of "What can we do?" among the group.

Finally, Muriel asked, "What about self-publishing?" Again, the room went quiet for several moments.

"David, do you have any money?" Jonathan asked.

"What's it cost to self-publish?" David asked.

"No, I don't mean that. Do you have any assets someone could come after in a lawsuit?"

"Not really. I guess our net worth is the balance on our Visa. But because of that, I don't think I could come up with the cash to self-publish."

"If you are sued, you could lose whatever profits come from the book," Jonathan warned.

"I don't care about that. I just want this story out," David said.

"I'd contribute to your book," Muriel volunteered.

"Me too," Walter said.

The rest of the group declared they would chip in to get David's book self-published and marketed. Even Brianna, the much maligned receptionist, offered to help.

"I couldn't put any company funds in, but I have some personal savings and this story has to get out one way or the other," Jonathan said.

David looked around the room at all the people who were willing to help him and felt justifiably guilty. "Folks, I'm very sorry how I came in here this afternoon. I wasn't going to hurt anybody. Actually, I took the bullets out of my gun this morning. And I don't think editors are assholes or receptionists are brain dead, never did, I just didn't know what to do next."

"Desperate times call for desperate measures. In the short term, it sounds like we have a major issue here relative to David's protection. Can everybody stay here for a while and utilize your writing skills?" Jonathan asked.

The group nodded in unison.

"Okay," Jonathan said. "Let's divide the manuscript into equal sections and make notes in the margins, and do some group editing and proofreading. I'll check to make sure we don't have any continuity issues. Don't change the storyline, character development, or back stories. If there any direct accusations of any individual or company, highlight those, and we'll make sure there is some documentation or supporting data for footnotes. Brianna, bring in your laptop and scanner and as we finish pages, we'll give them to you, and you can put them into a new PDF document.

I'm going to call a friend of mine who owns a printing company, then some marketing and cover design people I know, and see what kind of scheduling lead time we have to have in order to get this thing printed...quickly."

"What can I do?" David asked.

"How much sleep did you get last night?"

"About two hours," David admitted.

"I think you've done enough. There's a shower and a twin bed in the next office. Go get cleaned up and get some rest. I'll bring in some clean clothes for you. It looks like we're about the same size."

David initially looked relieved as he glanced around the room at those willing to help him. But then his paranoia emerged as everyone stared at him. A look of fear came over his face.

Jonathan saw the look. "David, we all realize what you have been through, but you can trust us. Let us help. Even being a small part of this kind of story, your story, is every writer's dream, and we would very much like to help you."

"Jonathan's right," Muriel said. "I've been looking for something like this to be part of for a long time. I want to help too."

The rest of the eclectic group around the table nodded, gave a thumbs-up, and smiled at David in support. David saw their enthusiasm and was grateful, but the exhaustion he had felt the night before was coming back and at that moment was overwhelming his brain function.

The two hours of restless sleep he had gotten in the closet the night before had only temporarily fought off the collective effects of days of lack of rest, pain, injury, fear, and worry. All he could do in response to the support of those around the table was to shake everyone's hand as he left the room.

"Thank you," David said hoarsely.

CHAPTER 51

DAVID STOOD IN THE SHOWER with his face only inches away from the hot water stream. For a moment he felt he actually went to sleep. He spread his arms out to support himself in case he began to fall.

As the healing liquid washed over him, the steam rose and caressed his body. It was like he was being enveloped by a warm, wet medicinal blanket. After several minutes he felt the pain of the deep cuts, gouges, bruises, and scrapes slowly abate. It was an intoxicating feeling, and for nearly fifteen minutes he remained motionless and allowed himself to be healed in the soothing warmth.

Slowly, his brain began to reengage, and he realized he had been lucky. He could have easily ended up like James, Gino, and Marie. That realization made him look back through the glass shower door, and for an instant he felt vulnerable and the paranoia returned. He tensed like he was ready for a fight. But the feeling passed, maybe because he was just too damn tired to fight, even if he had to.

As he continued to stand under the hot, soothing water, something else entered his brain and took root that he had not thought of before. What he and Syd had learned and faced over the previous weeks and months was far more than just fodder for getting a damn book published. It had become a mission to tell the truth. And as corny as it sounded, to protect their country. Again.

Like other missions they had been on, this one required determination, planning, execution, and the willingness to see the mission through to its conclusion, no matter the cost. For the first time in years, he felt like he was in battle again. He felt like a soldier again. Despite all the pain, the paranoia, and the fear, for some bizarre reason it felt good and comfortable and right, like he was back doing what he should be doing.

After another twenty minutes in the shower, David limped to the bed, lay down on his back, and stared up at the ceiling. He could hear the muted voices from the conference room as the group of writers pored over his work and quietly talked among themselves. He felt the urge to get up and help them. Then the urge passed, and he drifted off into a comalike sleep where he encountered an amused and younger Syd.

CHAPTER 52

"I'VE DECIDED TO DRAFT YOU for the summer," David announced to a less than enthusiastic Syd.

"What if I don't want to be drafted? What if I want to be a free agent for the summer?"

"What?! If you make such a regrettable decision, then you'll miss out on the best three months of your life. As a result, I'd feel very sorry for you to have lost an opportunity to be with such a charming, intelligent, witty, incredibly handsome future admiral. Such disastrous decision making would inevitably and most assuredly ruin what otherwise could be a very bright future for you and our children."

After several seconds of staring at David in awe of his incredible ego, Sydney said, "You realize you're completely full of shit, don't you?"

"Well, I must admit I have been told that in the past from time to time, but I prefer to ignore the negativity of my detractors and focus on a path of internal self-improvement without input from others."

"It's not working."

The conversation had taken place nearly twenty years earlier at the Oak Brook Mall outside Chicago where Sydney and David worked as models for a clothing store in the affluent suburb. They had both graduated from high school that summer and had eyed each other from afar before David decided that "the hot, dark-haired chick" had earned his "First-Round Draft Pick" status for the summer before college. A status Sydney was less than impressed with.

"If you want to go to a Cubs game or something, maybe I'll decide if we can have a second date or not," Syd advised.

"I'm a Sox guy, but I guess I can stand Wrigley for one day."

That rocky start to a relationship was not enhanced when David talked about himself for three nights in a row before Syd was finally able to get a word in edgewise. When she did, she informed David she would be going to Annapolis, and if he in fact enlisted in the Navy after college, which was his plan, it was possible she could be his commanding officer at some point in the future. "I'd have to call you, sir?"

"Female officers are called ma'am. Not sir."

"That's okay. I could handle it. I mean you are pretty smart."

"Thanks. Did you know officers in the Navy can't date each other unless they get C.O. approval?"

"Maybe I should join the Air Force."

"Maybe I should go to West Point, I got accepted there too."

"Now you're just showin' off."

Sydney loved David's sense of humor but learned he was more than a glib, good-looking jock. He was smart, had depth, in addition to being kind and considerate. He was also an excellent writer, something Syd discovered when she found a binder of short stories he had written over the years. He was embarrassed when Syd said she had found and read some of them in his garage when working on the old 1967 Pontiac GTO he had bought that summer. "Wow David, these are good. You should be a writer."

"Oh, that's just some stuff I wrote for fun."

"No David, these are really good. You should work on your writing; you have a flair for it," Sydney said.

Growing up in suburban Chicago, Syd was an average American girl in some ways but in other ways she was anything but average. While she liked dolls, had crushes on members of boy bands, sometimes wore black lipstick, and loved sleep-overs with her friends, she was in many ways quite different from those same friends. Sydney was fascinated by math, science, aviation, sports in general, and the Chicago Cubs in particular. Those interests eventually isolated her from many of her girl-friends as she grew older.

She also had a very well developed, albeit somewhat sick sense of humor compared to her friends, along with a definitive sense of right and wrong. On more than one occasion as a kid, she had willingly jumped in the middle of schoolyard scuffles if she thought someone was being unfairly picked on. Even the bigger boys learned not to mess with Sydney especially after she earned a brown belt in Tae Kwon Do when she was only eleven-years-old at the insistence of her mother, who warned her she had to learn to defend herself since she had no brothers or father around to stick up for her.

Sydney's father had left her and her mother when Sydney was only three, and she never saw him again. As she grew older, even the snippets of memories she had about him faded until only the few photographs her mother had of him indicated that he had even existed in her life.

Sydney and her mother had a strong bond that transcended the normal mother/daughter relationship. They always had each other's back. They were a close-knit team that fought through a series of low-paying jobs for her mother, which meant that Syd was often alone in the house.

Her mother warned her not to waste that time. She told her to use it to study the science and math subjects in which she already excelled. "You can be whatever you want to be, but you have to get the grades. You have to be the best, or someone will snatch your dreams away. Don't let them," her mother said repeatedly. The words "Don't let them" became Syd's mantra.

When Sydney delivered a stirring high school valedictory address on the subject of "Not Letting Other People Take Your Dreams Away," her mother held back her tears, not wanting Sydney to think what she had accomplished was anything out of the ordinary or not expected from her. But when she was accepted to the US Naval Academy, her mother lost it and burst into tears when Sydney showed her the formal letter of acceptance.

Her mother used that event to announce that she was getting married to a successful attorney and former Army colonel from Florida and would be moving to Boca Raton as soon as Sydney went off to the Academy. He was a man whom Sydney had met several times over the years, even though he had been introduced as only a "friend."

Sydney had intuitively known better, and she very much liked the idea that her mother would no longer be alone and would be taken care of by a kind, caring man when Sydney was off at college and then onto her tour of duty.

During the summer between her high school graduation and entering Annapolis, Syd returned to her modeling job at an upscale clothing store at the Oak Brook Mall that catered to the country-club set in the Chicago suburb. Syd had started modeling in the fifth grade. She never liked modeling but did like the pay and the free time it afforded her to work on science and rocket experiments during the summer.

As that summer wore down and David prepared to head east to NYU and Sydney to Annapolis, both assumed their summer romance would fade when the leaves turned and classes began. In fact, it did. But they stayed in touch once in a while via email and remembered each other's birthdays. Then for some reason, all contact ended after both had graduated college and each was simply a fond memory in the mind of the other.

All that changed when Sydney saw David during Hell Week, the week David almost quit his dream of becoming a Navy SEAL. On assignment from her Special Ops training in Pensacola, Sydney was detailed to visit the Great Lakes Naval Station to see how the wannabe SEAL candidates dealt with their last few days of Hell Week before the even more daunting BUD/S training began.

Among the dirty, exhausted group of young men who were being challenged as they had never been challenged before, Syd saw a familiar face. Since she had last seen David, he had received his bachelor's degree from NYU with a major in creative writing, enlisted in the Navy where he qualified for flight school, and then decided to get his ass kicked and apply for the SEAL program just for fun.

The fact was David didn't really think he would make it. But as the worst week of his life wore on, with no end in sight, something happened. A competitive spirit kicked in for David when he looked around the room after a particularly grueling day and saw some tough, determined guys trying to take something he had suddenly decided he desperately wanted.

He fought through the pain, the cold, the exhaustion, the hunger, the sore feet, the aching body, and his initial hatred for the SEAL instructors who tried their best to make the men quit. They even offered a comfortable bed, a warm meal, hot chocolate, and a hot shower to men who were freezing in forty-five degree water, out of their minds with fatigue and dizzy from lack of food. David refused to quit. He told himself he would die first.

He had not seen Syd when she had visited Great Lakes that day, but a week later he received an unexpected email from her congratulating him on his major accomplishment. While his response to Syd was perfunctory, David was thrilled to have her back in his life, at least via the internet, and pledged to himself, "I'm going to marry that woman someday."

Having lost his father and mother while still in junior high school in a car accident, David had, with the exception of some aunts and uncles he lived with before he went to college, been alone for over ten years. During some self-analysis one night alone in his room, after four beers and a pizza, he concluded that was why he joined the Navy in the first place. He wanted to be part of something, be on a team that mattered. Be part of a family and do something important. He wasn't quite sure what that was but concluded he would know it when he found it.

Yet he knew he didn't want to be alone forever, and he had never forgotten that summer with Sydney. He understood that she was out of his league in just about every way possible, but his ego, of which there was a significant amount, had compelled him to "go for it that summer" reasoning that all she could say was no to him "drafting her." To his surprise she didn't.

Despite all the accomplishments--graduating from NYU, joining the Navy, becoming a SEAL, and getting his "wings", David realized something was missing in his life, and he felt he knew *who* that missing piece was.

And now, because of all his achievements, nothing, not even Sydney, seemed out of his reach. He finally felt he may have *earned* Sydney not through bravado or looks or charm, but through something more important. Something Sydney could understand. Despite all that, Sydney still intimidated David like no SEAL instructor ever could.

For the next several months as David completed his final training and Sydney moved into her Special Ops responsibilities, their only communication was via email and an occasional phone call. It was Sydney who finally suggested they meet in New York for dinner and a play to get reacquainted. The evening turned into a three-day weekend and by Monday night both knew they wanted to be together for the rest of their lives.

When they returned to their respective bases, they learned the Navy had other plans for them, at least for the time-being. They were both going to be assigned to the Coronado Naval Facility near San Diego. During their tours of duty, they had to maintain a strictly professional relationship so no one could know they had been dating. Or would know.

After their final mission, they left San Diego, headed back to New York, and got married as quickly as they could. On their honeymoon to Miami, David said, "I told you I was going to draft you."

Sydney replied, "God, you were easy. I picked you the first time I saw you in a sport coat. It took a while, but I got my man."

CHAPTER 53

IT WAS TWELVE HOURS BEFORE David's eyes opened, then closed, then opened wide again. He was still on his back in the exact same position as when he had fallen asleep the night before. He tried to move, but his arms and legs felt frozen. After several tries, he finally got his left arm to move and used it to lift his right arm. After several more minutes, he got his toes to wriggle, then his ankles, and finally both legs reluctantly showed signs of life.

After taking a bodily inventory and determining everything was working albeit sore as hell, he realized there was no sound coming from the conference room. In fact, the office was dark and utterly silent. He also realized he had to pee. He swung his feet off the bed onto the floor and saw a note on top of a stack of clean clothes left by Jonathan.

David, we got a lot of work done tonight and I think we may have a fast-track path to get your book "out there" within 2-3 weeks. Stay as long as you wish, even all night. I alerted security you might be leaving late so don't worry. Call me on my cell over the weekend to discuss next steps. PS, I hope you don't mind but I took some precautions to see to it you'll stay safe. Jon.

Using both arms to lift his aching legs, David got up from the bed but grimaced when he finally stood up and remembered it had only been thirty hours since he jumped from a moving Ford and bounced several times on an off-ramp.

After his much-needed trip to the bathroom, where Jonathan had provided toothpaste, a toothbrush, deodorant, extra-strength Advil, and Neosporin, he painfully put on the clothes that had been left for him. He concluded that Jonathan wasn't, after all, the aloof, tight-ass, corporate jackoff that David suspected him to be the day before. Hell, he was actually kind of a likable guy, and David was grateful for what Jonathan and the rest of the group from the conference room had done for him.

He walked from the office/bedroom into the now empty and dark conference room and considered looking for the donut box but decided he wasn't that hungry. After he flipped on one row of lights, he saw his manuscript neatly stacked at the end of the table. Next to it was his bullet-less pistol. After he gathered up his stuff and shoved the pistol into his pocket, he moved into the main office that would lead to the lobby.

Through the office windows he saw the sun beginning to rise in the east. He checked the clock on the wall and saw it was 6:35 a.m. As he moved to the door, he heard a voice from the back of the room. "Hi, David. Get your beauty rest?" David froze at the sound of the voice and instinctively reached for his pistol. "You and your wife have this thing for guns with no bullets, don't you?"

In the semidarkness of the room, David saw the ominous-looking figure of Detective Ernie Simmons, the NYC detective who had investigated the deaths of the two goons who had broken into David and Syd's apartment and paid with their lives.

Ernie was sitting/slumping in one ugly chair and had his feet propped up on another. Through the window leading to the lobby, David saw three other men who lounged on the chairs obviously trying, without much success, to get some sleep.

"C'mon David, I checked out your little toy there. It's not loaded. So, just have a seat and relax." Ernie said.

"Jesus Christ, is everyone in this country on the take?" David said disgustedly as he flopped down in a chair.

"Hey, times are tough David, and a guy has to make a living. You need to be more understanding of your fellow man."

"Now what? Another ride in the trunk to Long Island?"

"I don't like leaving the city all that much. Let's stay here and have a conversation, just you and me."

"Sure, why not? Hey, you know your buddy from DC got flattened by a semi a couple nights ago."

"What buddy from DC?"

"That cop."

"You mean the one from DC?"

"Yeah, who'd you think I meant?" David asked.

"I never called him."

"I thought you met him at Penn Station, and he gave you some stuff."

"Nope, like I said I never called him. How'd he get squished?"

"Big fucking semi."

"Tough. Really squished, huh?"

"Flatter than hell."

"I never called him because a friend of mine down in DC said he was kinda rotten. When I heard that, I never bothered to call him." Ernie said.

"Then why are you and your goon squad here?"

"Hey, easy big boy. Those are good guys out there. Not much to look at but they got your back in a tough spot."

"Then you're not here to kill me?"

"Guess we could if you really want us to, but Mr. Marshall called and told me your story, including what you told him happened at your apartment. I guess you mentioned my name to him. Anyway, I told him in addition to being a writer, you were kind of a hero too."

"I'm just a writer and cab driver. No hero."

"I did some investigating with some friends of mine and heard you were a fucking hero in the Navy. A SEAL, huh? Chopper pilot, too?"

"Where'd you hear that?"

"I'm a fucking cop...I get to see and hear all kinds of shit."

"Yeah, I was a SEAL and I flew."

"I called some other friends of mine and..."

"Sounds like you have lots of friends."

"I'm a real friendly guy. Anyway, I called these friends of mine at the Pentagon and they told me stuff."

"Really? What kind of stuff?"

"Pretty interesting info. Want to guess what they told me?" Ernie asked.

"Not really into guessing games."

"They said you were one of those guys."

"What guys?"

"You know, one of those guys who..."

"Your friends at the Pentagon should learn to keep their mouths shut," David said.

"I was a Marine, saw some tank action in the first Iraqi war. Always wanted to get Saddam's ass," Simmons said.

"Semper Fi."

"Yeah, I really miss it sometimes. You the shooter?"

"We were all the shooter. You know how it is...it's a team sport."

"Yeah, I know."

"So, what now?" David asked.

"Me and my boys are gonna stay with you for a few days just to make sure the bad guys don't come lookin' for you again," Ernie said.

"I was supposed to head to Florida late yesterday and go see Syd and her family. I'm worried about them."

"I hope you don't mind, but I took the liberty of calling Syd myself when you were getting your beauty rest. I told her what had happened yesterday and that I thought you needed some sleep. I also called a long-time buddy of mine who does some private work in South Florida. I asked him to check in with Syd to make sure she and her family are okay. He's a good guy and will look out for them."

"Thank you, that's a huge relief. I appreciate you taking the time to do that, Ernie."

"No big deal. Jonathan told me about your story and from what I understand, it's something people need to hear. Maybe it is a good idea for you to go down to Florida for a couple weeks, get healed up, and figure out what we do next."

"Jonathan said it will take at least two weeks to get the book printed and some more time for marketing but even then we may not attract any readers."

"I have a real good friend at MSNBC," Ernie said quietly. "I'll give her a call.

CHAPTER 54

MSNBC Studios, 30 Rockefeller Plaza, Manhattan, April 2013

THREE WEEKS LATER, A TANNED, healed, and rested David sat in a green room at Rockefeller Center in New York City with a Republican congressman from Indiana. "So, you're an author, huh?"

"Yes sir" David said.

"So who's your publisher?"

"I self-published."

"No shit. Get any distribution?"

"Haven't yet. Kind of hoping after tonight..."

"Be careful of Matthews. He'll try to cut your balls off."

"I'll be careful."

"I'm running in a special election, but I really don't even need to be here since I'm up by eight points."

"Really? Who told you were ahead by that much?"

"All the polls. And you have to admit those damn things are accurate."

"Oh, yeah, that's what I hear."

"What's your book about?"

"It's about how our political system has been completely overtaken by a group of people who have undermined our presidential elections from 1952 to the present. And how that group decides who is going to be president years in advance and sells that information to the highest bidders. It's also about how these people murder anyone who tries to get this story out that would allow the American people to know that they have been fucked over for nearly seventy years and will continue to get fucked over until they do something about it."

After several moments of not quite comprehending what he had heard, the congressman said, "Holy shit, I certainly hope your book is a novel."

One of the producers of the show entered the green room to deliver some bad news.

"Congressman, I'm afraid you will have to come back another time. Mr. Dawson will be our only guest tonight in our final segment."

"What the fuck?! You mean I'm getting bumped? By a guy who self-published?"

On the set of *Hardball*, Chris Matthews spoke with David for several minutes before going on the air. "I read your book. I sure hope you know what you're doing, what you're getting yourself into."

"I'm pretty sure I know."

"I thought at first it was a novel."

"Actually, I almost wrote it that way."

"When did you decide to make it nonfiction and a tell-all book?"

"When I decided I didn't care if I got sued or didn't make any money."

"This stuff will be tough to prove, you know."

"We have documentation. Written proof."

"That's not always enough."

"It'll have to be."

"Hope you have lots of cash for all the legal bills you're going to get."

"We've had a number of attorneys step up to offer pro bono services once they read the story."

"You know what this book will mean to your life, don't you?"

"I'll be able to get a good seat at a Mets game?"

"You'll be the most famous man in America... for ten minutes. Some people will love you and some will hate you. And forget about going to a Mets game."

"There's always cable."

"If your claims are proven, this country will never be the same, you know."

"Yes, it will. We'll just fix the problem and move on like nothing happened, or it will all be ignored and we'll still move on." David said.

"There's a rumor you were on the raid that..."

"Chris, if you bring that up, I'll walk off this set," David said firmly.

"I understand," Chris said.

"Ten seconds, Chris" the stage manager announced.

CHAPTER 55

IN A MANHATTAN HIGH-RISE office conference room twelve blocks away, Connie sat in her office suite with the TV on in the corner. Three men in expensive suits sat around her and stared at their cell phones in silence. In addition, there were three NYC lawyers with yellow pads and pens at the ready. They too sat in silence comforted by the knowledge they were each being paid $1,200 an hour for their valuable services. From the screen they all heard, *Let's play Hardball.*

As Connie watched the first three segments of the show and waited for David's appearance, she thought back to when she had joined the family business in 1984. Things were different then. It was far easier to make the numbers work. Fewer computers, no cable talk shows, no internet, and despite Watergate a decade earlier, fewer reporters snooping around looking for something. Anything.

Two years before her grandfather died, when Connie was still a graduate student at Cornell, and after earning an undergraduate degree at Wellesley, he called her to the three-hundred-acre family estate in Greenwich, Connecticut, to have what they had come to call "their chat." Those chats had been going on for years, and Connie always looked forward to spending an afternoon with the old man on the huge flagstone patio that overlooked a forty-acre private lake and nine-hole golf course.

She would listen to him talk about what had happened in the world of politics back in the thirties, forties and fifties before "we got a handle on things," was how he put it.

Her grandfather had served in WWI and was as patriotic a man as she had ever seen. He truly loved his country, but he was also a pragmatic, and successful businessman. He combined those passions to create an enterprise that catered to both.

It was never his intention to undermine the Constitution by his actions to select the president, despite what the voters thought they wanted. To the contrary, his deeply held conviction was that he was instead protecting the Constitution, a document he so revered that he carried a small version of the document in his coat pocket every day of his life for as long as Connie had known him.

He also sincerely believed he was protecting the citizens of America from themselves. He often invoked the sentiment from Jesus Christ himself to describe what he felt was his responsibility: "Father, forgive them; for they know not what they do."

He believed there would be a time in the future when American citizens could be trusted with something as important as selecting a president, but given what he saw every day on TV and in the papers, that time was still decades if not centuries away. So, in the meantime he would see to it that his beloved country was safe and secure under his watchful and protective eye.

He dealt with the seeming incongruity of what he was doing and what the framers of the Constitution had written by saying that the document was indeed "perfect." It was the hoi polloi that remained wanting. "The Constitution and the men who wrote it were just ahead of their time," he had often said to anyone who would listen.

He had told Connie on more than one occasion: "Someday we will have an educated population capable of making decisions that will impact the entire world. Until that time, we will continue to protect them from themselves and carefully select people, even a woman someday, who will effectively guide this country. To do any less would be treasonous."

Connie bought it. All of it. When her father died at a young age, devastating her grandfather, it was Connie who was groomed to take over the family business, maybe even run for president someday.

Until that time. she would learn how the numbers worked because the numbers were everything. She had flourished in college taking all the statistics and math classes she could find. But at the insistence of her grandfather, she also got a master's degree in political science and found that she loved the machinations of government, the day-to-day infighting, and the never-ending battles that she soon learned were more for show than substance.

She also concluded, during her final year at Cornell, that if she was going to someday take the reins of her grandfather's firm, she would have no time for a husband and a bunch of kids who would do nothing but slow her down and divert her attention. If she was going to truly protect her country, she would need to devote her undivided attention. Besides, as a beautiful, wealthy, New York socialite, she could have all her physical needs met by both men and women whenever she wanted. And she wanted those needs met on a regular basis.

Connie learned at an early age that most of what happened in Washington was indeed a grand performance put on by actors as accomplished as any in Hollywood. She recalled hearing the line, "Washington is Hollywood for ugly people, and Hollywood is Washington for stupid people." She believed it.

So when she learned the truth about the family business, that truth was in fact confirmation of what she had seen in action from the time she was a little girl and her family entertained hundreds of famous politicians over the years in their mansion in Georgetown. All those famous people were just actors to her. They all played a role in a colossal puppet show that her grandfather controlled with strings of power that circled the globe.

As she waited for David to be interviewed by Chris Matthews, she believed "this too shall pass," but she also knew that she would do whatever was necessary to protect the business she had been tasked with leading. She would also protect the country from a foolish writer who would put the country at risk by attempting to corrupt a system that had been put in place by genuine patriots who looked to her to perpetuate what had been so successfully constructed over the decades.

CHAPTER 56

"WELCOME BACK TO HARDBALL. OUR final guest tonight is David Dawson, the author of a book titled STAT$, as in statistics, that is so explosive that I questioned whether it was a novel or a true story based on facts and evidence. If this story is real, and if proven true, then this country's elections over the last sixty plus years have been manipulated and the outcomes determined by a small group of wealthy business people who have, in essence, selected our presidents for us."

Chris turned from the camera, looked at David, and continued. *"Mr. Dawson, these accusations you lay out in your book are very disturbing and, forgive my saying so, almost impossible to believe. You are quite literally asserting that every election in this country since 1952 has been rigged."*

"I never said the elections themselves were rigged, Chris. I said the information the electorate has been given through the media and the internet to make their decisions regarding their vote <u>has</u> been rigged."

"Is there a difference?"

"Of course. The citizens of the United States got who they voted for every time since 1952. It's just that their decisions were based on information provided by four econometric forecasting organizations that conspired to misrepresent the data that allowed the media to disseminate that bogus information. Voters then absorbed that consistently repeated and inaccurate information, assumed it was accurate, and voted accordingly."

"How did these four firms you talk about in your book select who they wanted to be president?"

"It was, in fact, a painstaking process. In some cases, they would begin analyzing potential candidates decades in advance. They would rate and categorize an individual's strengths and wait until those strengths would be needed or could be taken advantage of predicated on national and international conditions."

"Were these firms political? I mean were they driven by party affiliation in their selection process?" Chris asked.

"No. In their eyes they were above political parties and in fact thought the two-party system was an antiquated and debilitating part of the election process. Instead, they saw their role in selecting a president as a solemn responsibility to provide what the country needed most in terms of leadership, knowledge, temperament, intelligence, and image at a given point in history."

"Can you tell us any specifics as it relates to their selection process? For instance, why would they pick Reagan over Mondale or Obama over McCain?"

"These people were always forward thinking. They looked beyond a single election and studied trends and issues that needed to be addressed years in advance. In terms of say Reagan over Mondale, that was all about America's declining power after the Nixon/Ford mess and then a weak Jimmy Carter. But even Carter served their purposes

at the time. They decided to put Carter in for one term to calm down the nation after Watergate. They saw him as a single-term president, kind of a placeholder, and started planning for Reagan even before Carter's inauguration."

"Why Reagan in 1980?" Chris asked.

"After Iran had humiliated the U.S. by taking hostages and then taunting us in front of the rest of the world, the group decided we needed a president who would in essence scare the rest of the world into seeing things our way. A man with an international perception of being a potential loose cannon with his finger never far from the launch codes. That was Reagan. And it worked. The day after he was elected, Iran backed down and turned over the hostages. Within a few more years the Soviet Union collapsed, and America had without question won the Cold War. Reagan was the right man at the right time in their eyes, and many would argue they were right."

"But wasn't it possible Reagan would have been elected anyway, even without the help of the group you are talking about?"

"Sure, but the people making those decisions had learned their lesson in 1948 when Truman upset Dewey. After that election, when all the polls proved to be wrong, this group did not take any more chances. They would flood the media with false statistics and negative stories about a competitor that would guarantee the victory of one candidate over another."

"What about Obama and McCain?" Chris asked.

"They of course wanted to capture the attention of the non-white voting block, and Obama was the perfect guy to do that. He was brilliant, urbane, sophisticated, low key, always under control, and realized he would have to become a kind of political Jackie Robinson. He did all that and served the vital role of breaking down that racial barrier for future non-white presidents."

"When did this group start looking at Obama as a potential candidate?"

They almost waited to select him until 2016 but McCain was already too old and they didn't want to take the chance that Obama could have stepped on some kind of political land mine between 2008 and 2016 that would have made it difficult for him to be accepted as president. Plus they saw the financial meltdown coming, and by his own admission, McCain knew nothing about economics. Finally, they knew Obama was not only brilliant, but he was a lot tougher fighter than people realized."

"Does this group also get involved in senatorial and congressional elections?"

"They didn't used to, but over the last two decades they have jumped into those elections in a big way. They also focus on the Electoral College after what happened in 2000 with Gore and Bush. They did not want Gore to win, but he almost did until they got the help they needed in Florida. By the way, that cost them $20,000,000 to ensure that Bush won. They also learned that controlling the House and Senate makes it easier on the policy front and given all the money that pours into those races, it created a whole new profit center for them."

"What have these firms gained by making the presidential selections?"

"*Power and money. But also in their minds, they have gained the peace of mind of knowing that a single unqualified president can't bring the country to its knees.*"

"*How did they monetize their selection of a president?*"

"*Knowing who is going to be President many years in advance is worth hundreds of billions of dollars to people who can benefit from that knowledge.*"

"*For instance?*"

"*Military contractors, unions, political parties, Wall Street, banks, foreign governments, multinational corporations to name a few. All those groups and more can make plans knowing who will occupy the White House years before the fact. They would know future tax rates, legislation, the makeup of the Supreme Court, treaties, interest rates, all of it. It's priceless information for sale at a very high price.*"

"*So, the groups you just mentioned pay the forecasting companies money to steer an election?*"

"*No, that's not the way it works. The forecasting groups go to the international banks, unions, and other entities I mentioned and say, "Look, we can tell you today with absolute certainty who is going to be president in four years or even eight years. If you would like that information today and begin your planning, pay us now." Once the money is collected, the forecasting groups have the funds needed to buy the media time and disseminate faulty data via social media where it is in turn absorbed by the voting public. Like I said, the forecasting companies sell that information for a price. A very steep price.*"

"*As spectacular as those accusations are, you also claim that people have been murdered, because of the information you've uncovered. Do you stand by those claims?*"

"*Yes, I do.*"

"*We are almost out of time here, but I can't help but ask what this group did regarding the assassination of JFK?*"

"*I have no specific proof of how that situation was addressed and don't want to spur any more conspiracy theories on the assassination that should be fully addressed with the release of files in October 2017. But suffice to say, when they selected Kennedy, they had hoped he would serve out two full terms, but his personal actions created the need for change. He was simply too great a risk.*"

"*Wow, that is a classic Washington non-answer answer. One last question. Before you wrote this book, what were you doing as a profession?*"

"*I was a cab driver.*"

"*And before that?*"

"*I was in the Navy.*"

"*Care to elaborate on what you did while in the Navy?*"

"*No.*"

Chris turned to the camera and said, "*Well, you've heard it. This explosive new book was written by a cab driver who found information in the back of his cab that challenges the very essence of our electoral process. I can hear the attorneys' calculators adding up the hours as we speak. Back in a moment with our panel.*"

CHAPTER 57

CONNIE SWITCHED OFF THE TV. One of the men in expensive suits had an observation: "We have to stop him, now."

A second well-dressed man agreed. "We need to do whatever it takes."

One of the attorneys had a suggestion. "We can get an order from a judge to stop the sale of the book until a court can respond to any suit we file."

Everyone one in the room turned to Connie for what the hell to do next.

"No. We do nothing."

"Connie, we can't let this go. We have to crush this story. Our people will demand it," Stephan said.

Connie pointed to the three lawyers in the room. "Gentlemen, thank you. I will await your further confidential recommendations. And invoices."

After the lawyers left the office, Connie got up and moved to the floor-to-ceiling windows that overlooked Fifth Avenue.

"We can't stop the book from being leaked; it's too late for that. And we can't stop him from talking, for now. But it will pass."

"Pass? This is going to outrage..."

"Outrage who? The Democrats? The Republicans? Our clients? The idiots voting? All they care about is their Social Security, Medicare, and special interests. Keep the checks coming and no one cares."

"But Connie, this guy will be on every talk show on TV and radio. He'll be doing internet interviews with the *Journal*, the *Times*."

"He'll just be selling books. So what?"

"I thought our friend from DC was going to..."

"He succumbed to a semi."

"There are plenty of others we can..."

"Don't be a fool. The man has given himself the best protection he can...fame."

CHAPTER 58

OVER THE NEXT YEAR, DAVID became a literary rock star. His appearances on Fox, CNN, MSNBC, *The Daily Show*, being interviewed by Stephen Colbert, Jimmy Fallon, even appearing on *Saturday Night Live*, and scores of local and regional radio and TV stations made his book an international best seller. He even went to Europe and Russia where he was a big hit in the Kremlin, which said they always knew democracy was so much bullshit.

As a result of the tons of free marketing he got from scores of media outlets, David received several seven-figure offers from large national publishers who all told him they always knew his book was going to be a hit, and by the way, did he have any more stories ready for publication? His six-book deal for a new author set an advance record.

But the deal he finally inked with a large publisher was predicated on Jonathan Robert Marshall being hired as a senior editor at that firm at a considerably higher salary than his previous position at Pegasus. The deal was further contingent on Jon being allowed to take his own private assistant with him a bright young woman named Brianna.

David also saw to it that every one of the people who helped him in that conference room that day, when he needed help most, received checks in the mail every quarter for their "partnership role" in the creation of *STAT$*.

Then as quickly as his book had become the source of seemingly endless conversation and 24/7 media coverage, the topic of how a handful of companies had been determining US elections for over sixty years passed from page one coverage in the *New York Times* to page six coverage in the *Des Moines Register*. It became old news.

Other stories that told of terrorist attacks, plane crashes, and a rising stock market emerged and grabbed the attention of the media and ultimately the public. Eventually, the claim of voter manipulation, fraud, and even murder surrounding the possible theft of a core element of American democracy became an afterthought.

Besides, the government said, there was nothing they could do about such a claim even if it was true, and furthermore, everything would be better now going forward since the government was now in complete and total control of the situation.

The fact was, some people believed David's story, and some did not. That lack of consensus and the resulting debate in the media and in bars across the country made plausible deniability by the four companies named in David's book sound reasonable.

Sure, there were files with some possibly incriminating memos. But those memos could have been faked. Or added to the file at a later time by James who could have been nothing more than a disgruntled employee who was possibly killed by some black teenagers during a robbery in a hotel in Washington, DC.

The irony of the whole story was that neither political party wanted to pursue it. Each cast doubt on the accuracy of the story in David's book. Each said such a story was more fiction than fact, and it was time to move on to bigger issues, like health care and infrastructure, and most importantly the upcoming 2016 election. Besides, no one wanted their election to office challenged or have doubt cast on it.

Yet there was the unavoidable issue of officially determining the guilt or innocence of those companies that had been accused of rigging the game. Of purposely disseminating fraudulent statistical information to the media and ultimately to the American public in order to make a buck and select presidents.

CHAPTER 59

TWO YEARS AFTER *STAT$* HAD become an international best seller, David testified in front of a Senate subcommittee. The senior senator from Georgia began the questioning.

"Mr. Dawson over the last two years how many copies of your book *STAT$* have been sold around the world?"

"I'm not sure."

"Is it closer to three hundred copies or three million copies?"

"Three million."

"Congratulations. And I understand you've been on the Best Sellers list for fourteen consecutive months, is that correct?"

"Fifteen."

"Forgive me. And you have two more books coming out this year?"

"Yes."

"So, it appears your book *STAT$* has made you very wealthy and very famous."

"Not as famous as you, Senator. And certainly not as wealthy."

Laughter erupted from the audience. The senator was not amused and glared at David.

"Mr. Dawson, why did you choose to write a nonfiction book as opposed to a novel?"

"Because I wanted to write the truth, not fiction."

"You say everything in your book is true."

"It is."

"Really? Yet after two years of bipartisan investigation by scores of governmental and private law enforcement agencies, at the cost of tens of millions of American tax payer dollars, not a single charge of impropriety has been filed against those firms and their senior management that you claim did everything from manipulating elections for decades to committing murder. How do you explain that?"

"Luck?"

When the audience laughed again, the committee chairman slammed down his gavel. "Order!" he said.

"Mr. Dawson, your rather cavalier attitude about having created such an uproar in this country over a book filled with false accusations, innuendo, and outright lies is in my mind criminally negligent and irresponsible." The Senator stated.

"Then senator, given your strong feelings on the matter, I would suggest you begin criminal proceedings against me immediately. Or perhaps

I should begin a slander charge against you for what you just falsely accused me of."

"I think you have already gotten far more press than you deserve, and I have no intention of giving you even more during the course of a trial," the senator said dismissively.

"Senator, there is not one accusation, one account, one paragraph or one line in my book that is false, misleading, or exaggerated. The fact that the government has, by all accounts, conducted a tepid and half-hearted investigation into this story is proof to me that it did not want to find the truth. That the government is, given its lack of aggressiveness in pursuing this case, admitting its indirect complicity in a cabal that has been perpetuated on voters in this country for over sixty years."

"Mr. Dawson, that is a totally outrageous and unfounded statement. Are you actually accusing this body of being complicit and criminally involved in disenfranchising the American electorate of this country for six decades? If so I..."

"No sir, I am not. What I am accusing this body and others of is being lazy. Not being students of history, not paying attention, and most of all not giving a damn when things don't make sense. Not challenging others when the math does not add up."

"What makes you think the government would in any way benefit from the dissemination of inaccurate data from four companies that it has on a bipartisan basis relied on for all this time?"

"Senator, you're running for reelection this year, is that correct?"

"Yes."

"And what do the polls say your chances are for reelection?"

"I have a ten-point lead as of last week."

"Congratulations. With that kind of lead, is it safe to say it's easier for you and your campaign to raise money for TV and radio spots than it would be if you were ten points behind?"

"Yes, but..."

"Further, with that kind of lead, your party can invest their capital resources into other races where the numbers don't look so good. The fact is, the ten-point lead you enjoy gives your party the latitude to help other senators and congressmen who are struggling, is that correct?"

"Yes, but that is how the system works. It has always worked that way."

"Senator, how do you really know you have a ten-point lead? And how would it change your strategy and the strategy of your party if, in fact, you had only a one-point lead? Or even trailed?"

"Are you saying I don't have a ten-point lead?"

"No senator, I am not saying that. What I am saying is you don't really know what your lead is either. Or even if you would actually have a lead if your potential voters were getting accurate, unbiased information and numbers. The reason you don't know is the polling companies asking all the questions of all the citizens to come up with those numbers are speaking with people who have read fake data for months. Based on that fake data, the pollsters get the information that those preparing that information *want* them to have."

"I, for one, believe I do in fact have a ten-point lead and I further believe you are, Mr. Dawson, attempting to undermine my election and the elections of other senators and congressmen and even the president of the United States with your scurrilous and unfounded accusations in an effort to sell books. Sir, you should be ashamed of yourself."

"Senator, would you feel the same way if the polls said you were trailing by ten points?"

"Mr. Chairman, I have no further questions for this witness."

After several more hours of similar questions and answers, the Senate subcommittee adjourned. When David and Syd walked down the steps of the Dirksen Senate Office Building after the hearing, a large contingent of photographers and reporters blocked their path wanting to hear directly from David. Thirty feet away another group of reporters questioned Connie and her associates. Connie glared at David and Syd.

"With us here after David Dawson's testimony is Miss Constance Reynolds, whose firm was specifically named in Mr. Dawson's book as a major player in releasing false and misleading data. Miss Reynolds, while you and your company have been exonerated from any criminal liability in this case based on a lack of clear evidence, what do you say about the Senate and House establishing a permanent oversight group of bipartisan statistical analysts that will examine all of your company's work in the future?"

"We have absolutely nothing to hide. We welcome any scrutiny the government would like to impose on our work. Although, I must say I think this is another example of classic government overreach into the private sector. We must wonder why the government would expend the resources to do so in this economy. Hopefully, the next administration will reconsider such actions."

"Miss Reynolds, will you and your group sue Mr. Dawson for libel and/or slander?"

"We are looking at our options," Connie said with a smile

"This is Linda Jordan with CNN. Back to you, Wolf."

Within steps of Connie's interviews, David and Syd also faced the press. A reporter from MSNBC asked, *"This is Sharon Kelly Roth reporting from Washington, Mr. Dawson, do you think you are going to get sued based on the allegations in your book?"*

"No, I don't."

"Why not?"

"Because a private investigation into my story would be too risky for the plaintiffs."

"Too risky?"

"They know we would welcome a more meaningful and aggressive investigation into this case. They also know I'm telling the truth. They want this to end. Based on those facts they won't sue, although I can always hope."

"Mrs. Dawson, we understand you and Mr. Dawson are expecting your second child early next year."

"Yes, and we are very excited."

"You have a little boy now?"

"Yes, he's almost two. His name is Gino."

"Mr. Dawson, one last question, do you think the government creating a watchdog group to oversee the numbers coming from the four companies you targeted will have any impact on their earnings?"

"Ask them."

A nearby FOX reporter wrapped up the coverage. "Well, there you have it, Shep. Nearly three years after of the release of a book that created such an uproar in this country and even around the world, the author of that book, David Dawson, leaves a Senate subcommittee hearing enduring the wrath of many senators on both sides of the aisle who claim he made up a story to undermine the credibility of our nation's most sacred institution, the US voting system. However, while there was no proof the four companies charged in the original indictment committed any wrongdoing, the rules have indeed been changed. These four companies will, at least for the term of the remaining administration, fall under an oversight group that will demand detailed supporting documentation for any statistical information generated by these firms. Shep, back to you."

After their interviews, Sydney and David passed by Connie who continued to hold court with a half dozen reporters around her. She glanced quickly at David, but just as quickly returned her attention to the media.

CHAPTER 60

Barnes & Noble Bookstore, Manhattan, 2016

A MONTH AFTER THE SENATE hearing, David still basked in the glow of his literary and television fame at a bookstore in midtown Manhattan.

Over two hundred people attended one of his book signings and listened to him recount what he claimed were the true, albeit in some cases, unproven facts in his book. He also promoted his two new books, which were also selling well. In the back of the room, Syd stood alone and took in the proceedings and from time to time said hello to many of David's adoring fans who recognized her from the numerous newspaper articles and her interviews on the cable news programs.

One of those fans approached Syd and introduced herself. "Hello, Sydney. My name is Millie Hough, pronounced h–o–w, and I met your husband…"

"Oh my God, Millie. It is such a pleasure to finally meet you." Sydney said as she warmly embraced the Mercedes-driving white haired octogenarian. "David has told me a hundred times everything you did for him that night. How you believed in him and took a chance. I hope you got the case of autographed books he sent you, the return of your gift, unloaded of course, and your loan to him."

"I sure did, and all that was very kind, but not necessary. You know, he has an honest face and I just knew that boy was telling the truth that night. You know I have given some of those books to the local schools and colleges and told them they should use them in a class to teach the kids about the real world and this country's politics."

While Sydney talked to Millie, David wrapped up his remarks and, after receiving a stirring round of applause, walked toward the two women with a smile on his face. "Millie, how's my best girl?" David asked as he warmly hugged her.

As David and Millie talked of the good old times on the Long Island Expressway, several other fans came up to Syd and offered congratulations on David's success. Syd was gracious in her sincere thanks for their support. After ten minutes of greetings and handshakes, a middle-aged man in a dark suit sidled up next to Syd and stood beside her for several minutes watching David interact with his fans. "That guy is a pretty good writer" he said.

"I think so," Sydney replied.

"I read his first book. Very interesting premise."

"Thank you."

"You're his wife, Sydney, right?"

"Yes."

"Wow, you must be very proud."

"Yes, I am."

After several more moments, the man leaned over near Syd's ear and whispered, "I have a message for you from Connie. She said she's going to have someone videotape that new baby girl getting cut out of you with a steak knife right before gutting that cute little boy of yours like a piglet. Then your tits are going to be cut off and mailed to your husband on one of his book tours. I have to say, I am looking forward to that assignment. Have a good evening, Sydney."

As the man turned to walk away, Syd grabbed him by the arm, looked him in the eye and said, "Please tell Connie for me that I truly believe everything you just said."

After staring into Syd's eyes for several moments with a surprised look on his face, the man finally walked away, left the store, and disappeared onto the street. Syd did not exhibit any response to his threat. Instead, she stood calmly near her chair and continued to politely meet and greet David's adoring fans until the bookstore was empty.

CHAPTER 61

"NICE EVENING," DAVID SAID TO Syd on the limo ride back to their high-rise condo after the book signing.

"Yes, it was. It was great to finally meet Millie in person. She is quite a lady."

"I invited her to join us for dinner next week when she's visiting Palm Beach."

"Great idea. I'm looking forward to getting to know her better," Syd said.

"I saw you talking to a bunch of other folks, anybody we know?" David asked.

"No, just a bunch of your fawning fans."

"Actually, I kinda like to be fawned over."

"I noticed. In fact, I especially noticed how you responded to the fawning of that tall brunette in the low-cut dress."

"You mean the one in the tight-fitting, emerald green Vera Wang dress, the one with the beautiful white teeth, long legs, two-carat diamond stud earrings, and bubbly personality?"

"Yeah...*her.*"

"I didn't notice her and have no idea who you're talking about."

"What about the blonde in the tight red sweater?"

"You mean Nicole from Soho? I mean, maybe that's her name... just a guess. No I didn't notice her either...very much."

Syd smiled and snuggled up next to David in the limo, "I guess I better get used to you being a rich, famous, handsome writer that certain unscrupulous women will fawn over from time to time. Wonder what I could do tonight to get your attention back on me?"

"Well, there is that *one* thing you do..."

"You mean that *one* thing that..."

"Yeah... that one."

"You know, that's just for special occasions."

"My agent told me STAT$ could sell four million copies before it's done. That's special."

"Big deal," Syd said dismissively.

"You're kind of hard to impress these days."

"I guess you're right. You've been a good boy lately. Maybe I could do that one thing tonight."

David smiled, shut the divider between the back of the limo and the driver, and decided he wanted to make out with his best girlfriend in private on the way back to their apartment. Syd really liked that idea, although she saved that special thing for later.

That night in bed, David was fast asleep while Syd stared up at the ceiling in thought and listened to the darkness. After nearly two hours, she finally got up and checked on Gino down the hall. She went into the already decorated bedroom for Maria and stared at her empty crib. When she returned to bed, she kissed David softly on the cheek, turned over on her side, finally closed her eyes, and at long last, slept soundly.

CHAPTER 62

THE NEXT MORNING AFTER BREAKFAST, David put on his workout clothes and readied for his daily trip to the gym. He reentered the bedroom and saw that Syd was still in bed and heard her emitting the slightest of snores. Not really a snore like foghorn, more like a kitten trilling. David thought it was a cute sound and smiled when he looked down at her.

The best thing about the success he was enjoying as a writer was the impact that success was having on Syd. She was able to quit her job, stop worrying about the light bill, plan on enjoying the kids, and do whatever she wanted to do. Compared to where they were just a few years earlier, David was happy he was able to provide the life to Syd he felt she had earned. She had stuck by him, encouraged him, and even kicked him in the ass a few times when he needed it. But she never, ever, gave up on him. Not once.

He got down on one knee next to her and kissed her on the forehead. Syd opened her eyes and smiled at David.

"Hey pregnant lady, I fed and changed Gino. We watched ESPN for a while, then Animal Planet. He really likes elephants. He's in the pen and good to go for a while if you want to sleep in."

"Thanks sweetie...but I've got to get up and get some things done. The sitter will be over at 10:00."

"Want to meet up for lunch?" David asked.

"I can't today, honey. I'm meeting some old friends from school, and we're going to relive our youth for a day."

"Really? Anybody I know?"

"Yeah, you know them all."

"Oh."

"We have some things that need taking care of."

"Are you sure?"

"I slept on it. I'm very sure."

"Can I...?"

"No, you can't. Go work out. I'll see you later."

David stared down at Syd for several moments then bent over and kissed her again. "How about we get a sitter tonight, go to a play, and get a pizza at Sam's?"

"Sounds like date night."

"It is. Tell our friends I said 'hi.'" David said.

"See you later, sailor."

After David left, Syd did her exercises focusing on stretching and yoga, then hit the shower.

Afterward, she dried her hair with a thick towel and pulled it back into a ponytail. She applied minimal makeup, put on a black leotard and Nike running shoes. After she pulled a dark blue sweater over her head, she went to the closet and selected an already loaded black gym bag. Ten minutes later she greeted the babysitter at the door, said hello, and kissed Gino good-bye.

Syd walked down the street with the gym bag over her shoulder. At the corner of Fifth and Madison she entered a black SUV. Inside were three men dressed in work overalls with Gotham Window Washing stitched on the back. They gave Syd a pair of overalls to put on. She nodded and slipped them on over her workout gear.

The driver of the SUV stated, "We have confirmation of presence of objective and a number. Here's an untraceable phone." He handed the phone, number, and a photo to Syd.

Syd nodded again.

They drove several blocks and as they approached the gate of the parking garage beneath a modern glass and steel office building, it opened without the driver taking a parking ticket.

Once inside the garage they parked near a service elevator and waited. After several minutes, one of the men received a text message, and the group of four exited the SUV and walked to the elevator which immediately opened after one of the men pushed the up arrow. The padded service elevator was empty.

After entering the elevator car, they were, within thirty seconds, delivered to the mezzanine level of the building. They exited and walked nearly fifty yards to an electric scaffold already attached to the west side of the building. After they loaded their gym bags, they attached a dark green tarp to the outside of the scaffold proudly advertising "Gotham Window Washing." The tarp would conceal any activity taking place on the scaffold from people in surrounding office buildings.

CHAPTER 63

CONNIE SAT AT A LARGE glass desk inside her office suite that overlooked the city, reading the *Wall Street Journal*. The sky was blue and clear, and she could have seen miles into New Jersey if she had wanted to, but she hated New Jersey. Always had.

She wore a newly purchased royal blue Armani suit, an off-white silk blouse, and black pumps. She checked her gold Rolex and realized it was time for lunch. She pushed a button on her desk; within minutes a man in a dark suit entered her office pushing a cart that held aluminum-covered dishes that contained a cobb salad, chicken consommé, lemon sorbet, and iced tea. Connie did not acknowledge the man who placed the food on her desk and left without saying a word.

Just as she was about to take a bite of her salad, her cell phone rang, she answered. "This is Connie."

"Hello, Connie. This is Sydney Dawson, David's wife. I believe you had someone deliver a message to me last night at the book signing. I wanted to reach out to you and make sure it was indeed a message directly from you."

"Well, this is a surprise, Sydney. How did you get my private number?"

"Oh, it wasn't that hard. I guess nothing is really private anymore, is it, Connie?"

"I suppose not. As to the message, yes, it was in fact from me but represented the feelings of many of my partners. You see, my partners are upset about the negative impact the book your husband wrote is having on our business. David is, in their eyes, a very naughty boy, and I am afraid they are demanding retribution."

"Interesting group of partners you have who would threaten children."

"I believe the term is collateral damage, Sydney."

"And David and I are also part of that collateral damage? And my parents?"

"I am afraid David's book has caused quite a stir with the wrong people. If you called to ask for me to intercede on you and your family's behalf, there is really nothing I can do."

"That's too bad."

"Well, perhaps David should have thought of consequences before he wrote his little book and..."

"Oh, I'm not talking about David's book. I'm talking about your apparent inability to stop the murder of my children, my parents, my husband, and me. I mean if you could stop it, or even wished to stop it, I might have a different view of things."

"Sydney, even if I could stop what's going to happen, and my dear, it is going to happen, I wouldn't. David needs to be punished for what he has done to my partners and what he has done to this country. Hopefully, others will learn from the misfortune you and your family will experience. But look at it this way, it is after all only two children. I doubt the world will mourn their loss."

"Perhaps not. But I wonder if the world would mourn your loss, Connie?"

"That sounds like a bit of a threat, Sydney. Is the diaper-changing housewife calling to threaten me?" Connie said with a laugh.

"First of all, I apologize for sounding vague. Usually, when I make a threat, there is little doubt in the mind of the person I am threatening. Good-bye, Connie."

CHAPTER 64

AFTER SYD HUNG UP ON HER, Connie went back to eating her salad but then stopped, picked up her cell, and dialed a number.

After his workout, David sat at his locker buttoning his shirt when his cell rang.

"Hello."

"Hello, David. It's your old friend, Connie. So nice to hear your voice. It's been way too long."

"Hello, Connie. Yes, it has been a long time. I meant to call and tell you how great you looked on national TV during the Senate hearings last month, but I've been so busy traveling, you know how it is."

"Of course, I can understand how hectic your *best-selling-author schedule* must be. And thank you so much for noticing my appearance. That is such a valued compliment coming from you. You know what they say about a tan and great clothes. And I must say you were looking much more prosperous at the hearings than the last time we were together."

"Selling a few million books can do that for a person."

"Don't forget, David, fame and fortune can be fleeting. Among other things."

"True. That's why I prefer to tell the truth about things and fame and fortune be damned."

"My, I marvel at how noble you are."

"You know me, once a boy scout, always a boy scout."

"Then you'll be happy to hear that your friends from the Senate and House have been dutifully looking over our shoulders every day now for the last two years. It's like having a never-ending tax audit. Every time I see one of those overpaid bean counters in our office, I can't help but think of you and remember a discussion we once had about patriotism and love of country."

"Oh, you'll get used to it, Connie. Who knows, at some point, maybe giving accurate information to the unwashed masses will actually appeal to you in some perverse way."

"David, I wonder, given the candidates I see lining up for 2016, if you will retain that smug Dudley Do-Right attitude if the wrong candidate should emerge from the pack of disturbing ineptitude I see every day and actually becomes this country's next president."

"As the old saying goes, men, or now women, 'rise to the office.'"

"Frankly, David, and with all due respect to a best-selling author, that is utter nonsense. But it is in keeping with other governments around the world in the twentieth century that believed such rot only to later rue such belief."

"I think we will get by."

"The fact is men or women don't rise to the office of president; they are prepared for the office of president. They are groomed. They are trained, even if they don't know they are being trained.

"And you believe you have some God-given right to be the groomers and trainers?"

"The people I now see seeking that office are laughably unprepared, and in one case, incredibly dangerous to this country. Thanks to people like you, a person like that could bring this country down to its knees and fundamentally change it to such an extent that it would never recover or ever be the same."

"I guess we won't know until we give it a try, will we, Connie?"

"David, you fool, we already tried that strategy and we got Truman, Hoover, Coolidge, Wilson, Taft, Harding, and a dozen others who nearly destroyed this country because they were not prepared. Not able to lead this great nation."

"I think this country will survive anyone that is elected by the voters, and I'm glad I was able to make sure that they get the correct information that will allow them to make their choices in the future, no matter how bad they might be."

"How high-minded and naive on your part, David. However, I have heard from various reliable sources around the world that since we are out of the selection process, at least for now, another entity has stepped into our place. An entity that does not have our best interests at heart and never will. If they get their way, and it looks like they very well could, this country will never be the same. I hope you like what you are likely to see."

"Would you like to tell me who or what this entity is? Sounds like a pretty good sequel to my book."

"Not now. Besides, I think you will learn soon enough." Connie said. "In fact, I have a feeling you will at some point in the future, perhaps the very near future, question your role and the impact that you and others like you had on this country. I fear you will soon see that one poor choice by the American people can set this republic back many decades."

"I doubt it."

"Then you're indeed a fool. You will recognize what I am saying is true when you see what happens with media coverage over the next decade. Foreign entities and their representatives will acquire multimedia organizations that will skew public opinion, and there will be no balance. No evaluation of who is capable of being president, who would protect this country, only unvarnished partisan politics enhanced by hate groups and the internet. It will be something even someone like you will lament."

"I'll take my chances."

"See that's the difference between you and the group of the true patriots I represent. We were not willing to take chances. Not with something as precious as our country. However, I did not call to debate political tactics and philosophies. I called to let you know that at the insistence of several of my partners, I was compelled to send an errand boy to your book signing last night."

"How nice. Hope he at least bought a book."

"I'm afraid not, but he did deliver a message."

"Really? I never got one."

"Oh, it was a personal message to that beautiful wife of yours."

David stood up next to his locker. "What kind of message, Connie?"

"Up close and personal, and I'm afraid a bit graphic in its content. But I assure you, very sincere, heartfelt and one that I would consider fair warning."

"What was the message, Connie?"

"I'm surprised dear Sydney did not relate it to you."

"What was the damn message, Connie?"

"It had something do with your little boy and soon to be little girl. And of course, a painful life lesson for Sydney. All of which you will see in full HD living color."

"Did he say the message was from you?"

"Yes, he did, and low and behold, I just had a call and a lovely conversation with your Sydney and confirmed the message she received last night was very sincere."

"What did you say to her?"

"David, did you really think you could get away with what you did? You cost very important people billions of dollars. They are rather upset with you and have long memories. They are looking to me for appropriate action. I'm afraid it is really quite out of my hands at this point."

"Where are you, Connie?"

"David, David, I expect more from you and your wife than threats when all I am doing is delivering you a simple message, a simple warning."

"Threats? I'm not issuing you a threat, Connie. I am offering *you* a friendly warning."

"I'm sorry, David, but you don't scare me."

"Connie, I'm definitely not the one you should be afraid of."

CHAPTER 65

CONNIE WAS A BIT SURPRISED when David hung up on her; that wasn't like him. In fact, she had been hung up on twice in only a few minutes. She didn't like not getting in the last word.

Not dwelling on the negatively and rudeness of others, Connie turned her attention back to her cobb salad and had just speared a piece of tomato with her fork when her west view of New Jersey was blocked by a window washer's scaffold that slowly rose in front of her. Given her fear of heights, Connie always marveled that people would select a job that required dangling hundreds of feet in the air every day in order to make a living.

As Connie stared with interest at the activity outside her window, the shortest of the four window washers had their face partially hidden by a baseball cap and turtleneck sweater that covered their nose and mouth. Without warning, the short one reached into their bag, pulled out an automatic weapon, and fired several shots into the double pane window, shattering it into a million pieces.

As the air pressure inside the office suite was released by the open window, a powerful gust of air blew papers around Connie's office like a Kansas tornado. It swirled and knocked over lamps, it removed artwork and framed civic citations describing Connie's deductible donations to charities, including children's aid, from her office walls. It swooped up the small fine crystal figurines off Connie's desk and sent them flying toward New Jersey.

Within seconds of the shots, three men in business suits armed with automatic pistols ran into Connie's office and were picked off one by one by the men on the scaffold. All were shot in the eye and chest.

Through all the breaking glass, the gunfire, and the swirling wind, Connie had not moved. She still held her fork in her hand with a piece of tomato at the end of it. She finally stood and slowly moved around to the front of her desk and began to tremble as the short one dressed in black leaped from the scaffold into the office and stared at Connie for several moments. Syd removed her hat, lowered her turtleneck collar and stared at a now shaking Connie. She finally dropped her fork as urine ran down her legs and formed a puddle on her plush off-white carpet.

Connie saw a red laser emit from the automatic rifle that Syd carried. Connie looked down and saw the red dot on her Armani suit. "Sydney...I..."

The first bullet struck Connie in the chest right between her breasts. A look of confusion came over her face as she looked out the window toward

New Jersey. Ironically, it was the last thing she ever saw as the second bullet went through her left eye and sent her sprawling backwards onto her glass desk where she lay with her legs spread and her remaining eye wide open.

After several seconds, Syd returned to the scaffold, which began its decent to the mezzanine level of the building. From there, the group of four went back down the service elevator, returned to the van, and exited the garage within ninety seconds. The guard gate had been conveniently left open to allow for easy egress. There was no charge for parking.

CHAPTER 66

AFTER HIS ABORTED CALL WITH Connie, David took a walk through Central Park. He was not quite sure what he should do next. He tried calling Syd, but there was no answer on her cell. He wanted to warn her, but he wasn't quite sure of what.

He knew what Connie and her crew were capable of and also knew what needed to be done. In the distance, he heard a series of sirens but that wasn't unusual for Manhattan. Was he being paranoid again? He remembered his conversation earlier with Syd. Had there been a planning meeting? They would meet to discuss the matter first, right?

As he walked past the park benches, dog walkers , and kids in strollers, David saw flashes of his old boss Gino with his throat cut. He remembered how the blood pooled at his feet. He remembered how Maria looked like she was asleep on the floor with all those stab wounds in her chest.

He could only imagine what had happened to James and knew what had almost happened to Syd. Something had to be done. To live any longer under such a cloud of fear and uncertainty was ridiculous. *Something had to be done.*

David sat down on the park bench and, using his writer's mind and military experience, crafted a flawless elimination plan. One that Connie might even understand. He felt better.

CHAPTER 67

AFTER HE ENTERED HIS CONDO lobby, David was surprised to see New York police detective Ernie Simmons, who was sitting on a leather couch reading the latest issue of *Sports Illustrated*. David saw him first. "Hey, Ernie, good to see you again."

"Hi, David. How are things?"

"Things are good."

"That's what I hear. Seen you on TV a few times. Loved the way you gave that Senator some shit back at those hearings."

"Just doing my duty for God and country."

"Hey, what have you been up to today?"

"Just worked out for a couple hours at my club, why?"

"Guess there were lots of people there?"

"Sure, like always. Why?"

"Oh, there was just a situation up at Connie's office building an hour ago."

"A situation?"

"Yeah, I don't have all the details yet, but it sounds like some window washers came up the side of Connie's building and in broad daylight shot she and her partners."

"No kidding? They all dead?"

"Yeah, they're all pretty dead. All shot the same way too. In the eye and the chest."

"Well, I'll be." David said.

"Yeah, but I guess she pissed off lots of people. Some folks thought she was guilty of murder and treason for what you accused her of. You know, subverting the Constitution for cash and all that kind of thing."

"I heard that."

"But some people think you made up all that stuff just to make a buck."

"Well, it's hard to please everybody, I guess."

"Yeah, but some of those people have long memories, and if it were me and I had plenty of money and a whole world to travel in, I'd probably consider a long trip somewhere. You know, a warm, beautiful place where you could write three or four books over a period of time, a long period of time, and stay out of the limelight for a while."

"Think so?"

"Yeah, I think so. You know, I'm a fucking cop, and I hear things, you know? And some of the things I've heard I don't like. So I think I'd work on that plan right away, I mean, if it were me and I had such a beautiful family and so many things to write about and live for. Yep, I'd work on that plan right away."

"You know, I think you could be right. Maybe getting away would be the best thing, for everybody."

"Glad we agree on that plan. You know I was talking to some friends of mine in the Department of the Navy, and they told me something I never knew."

"There you go talking with those friends of yours again."

"Yeah, they said you and Sydney served together. Is that right?"

"That's right. She was my C.O. for a while," David said.

"I'll be damned. What did she do in the Navy?"

"Can't really talk about what we did. You know, national security stuff."

"Oh sure, I understand."

"Hey, speaking of Syd, want to come upstairs and see her and Gino? I just spoke with her on the way over here, and she was fixing some lunch—you want to join us?"

"She's upstairs?" Ernie asked.

"Yes, just talked to her on the way in. Come on up and say hi, she'd love to see you."

"I'd like to, but I need to get over and check out the situation with Connie. I'll take a rain check though."

"You got it, any time."

Ernie got up from the couch and walked toward the door then stopped and turned back toward David. "You know what else my Navy guy said?"

"Not a clue."

"He said you weren't a very good shot."

"I wasn't that bad."

"Yeah, but not as good as Syd."

"Got me there. But then again, no one was as good as Syd. You know, she even had a nickname back in those days."

"A nickname? What was it?"

"Everybody called her A.O." David said.

"A.O.?"

"Yeah, you know, Annie Oakley."

Ernie smiled, nodded, waved at David, and walked away.

David entered the apartment and saw the babysitter was there with Gino. He chatted with her for a few minutes, paid her, and she left. Gino was taking a nap and as he often did, David stood by his bed and watched.

He loved to hear and see him sleep. The regular breathing, the occasional smile emanating from a two-year-old's dream, and how utterly content he was in his sleep.

After he left his son's room, David walked to the window and looked out. For the next hour he paced around the apartment and kept checking the clock on the wall. Finally, the door opened behind him. It was Syd.

"Hi," he said.

"Hi. How was your workout?"

"Good. How was your day?"

"Good. Met with some old friends of ours and talked about...you know, just stuff."

"How are those old friends?"

"Good. Real good. They said to say hello," Syd said.

"That's good. You know, I wish I could have..."

"That would have been a bit... awkward, don't you think?"

"Yeah, but still." David said.

"Don't worry...you're still on the team."

Sydney and David walked over and looked down at a still sleeping Gino.

"You know, I was just talking to Detective Simmons, and he had a suggestion."

"A suggestion?"

"Yeah, he thought it might be a good idea if we went on a trip."

"A trip? To where? For how long?"

"Pretty long time. A few years at least. You know, just get away from here," David said.

"Maybe he's right. Maybe it would be good for us and the kids to just go somewhere else. I'm pretty sure my parents would join us; you know we'd need babysitters."

"Good idea, always tough to find good sitters."

"How soon do you think we need to...?"

"Soon. Ernie strongly suggested we leave very soon."

CHAPTER 68

Montepulciano, Italy, September 2017

DAVID AND SYDNEY HAD DINNER in the center of the small town at what had become their favorite dining spot. It was a family-owned café nestled between an eight-hundred-year-old church and even older inn. The café had a limited menu but what it served consisted of fresh homemade pasta and a tomato sauce created from a garden in the rear of the establishment.

The bread and wine were impossibly good, and despite Syd's determination to lose the last three pounds after giving birth to Marie seven months before, she promised David she would jog an extra two miles the next day to make up for an extra piece of bread. And that small piece of tiramisu that was waiting just for her on the table.

"Your mom and the colonel seem to love it here," David said.

"I knew they would. Especially since they can watch the kids whenever they want."

"Do you miss home?"

"I did the first couple of weeks, but this is becoming home. Especially given what's going on back there now. Kind of hard to believe the things I'm seeing on cable," Syd said.

"I've been thinking about that, a lot."

"Figured you were."

"Syd, what if Connie was right all along?"

"Right? You've got to be kidding? She was a murderous thug who had undermined everything the country stood for."

"I'm not saying what she *did* was right at all. I'm just asking what if our country does not deserve the rights it has, at least for now. That while the principles are solid, maybe America is still too young to step up and do what it needs to do to protect the democracy."

"Are you saying you should have never written your book?"

"What if I hadn't?" David asked.

"Even if you hadn't written your book, James, Gino, and Marie would still be dead because those things happened before you wrote it."

"I've thought of that too. But Connie and her crew believed they were the true patriots. They did not see themselves as people who undermined the Constitution but instead protected it from the apathy and, in some cases, stupidity of the voters. They really believed guys like me were the enemies of the government and all it stood for. They felt they had an obligation to do whatever it took to protect the country from itself. They didn't see it as murder; they saw it as sacrificing a few for the good of the many."

"David, she was going to kill the kids, my parents, me, and eventually you for revenge, not for a cause. Don't second-guess for one moment what you did or what happened to that red-haired bitch."

"I'm not second-guessing what happened to her at all. If it hadn't happened the way it did, I was going to make sure it happened another way because I knew what she was capable of. All I'm saying is, what she and her group had done from 1952 until last November was in a way a sincere effort to protect this country from itself. Now I have to live with what happens going forward. Our country is going to fundamentally change as a result of my book, and based on what I'm seeing now we're off to a damn bad start."

"I guess you could say the training wheels are off the democracy," Syd said.

As David and Syd debated political science, two men entered the small café, sat down, ordered ravioli, and two glasses of merlot. The men noticed David and Syd, and one of them waved and asked, "Americans?"

"No," David said, "we're Canadians."

The men nodded and raised a toast to David and Syd.

Syd and David toasted back, then stared at each other for a few moments but said nothing.

"Yeah, I guess you could say the training wheels are off the democracy," David said in response to Syd's earlier comment. "I suppose it had to happen sooner or later. Hey, you gonna finish that tiramisu?"

"Touch it and you'll lose a hand, mister. Besides, you had yours already, and I want to savor mine and eat it real slow in front of you and watch you suffer."

Respecting a woman and her tiramisu, David sat silently, but inside he lusted after the chocolate delicacy that Syd ate as slowly as Italian law allowed until there was one small bite left on her plate. Syd scooped up the savory morsel on her fork in as taunting a way that a piece of dessert can be put on a fork, then smiled and moved it toward David.

He opened his mouth and awaited culinary ecstasy. As the fork slowly neared his lips, Syd snatched it away and gobbled up the tiramisu like one of those frogs with the long sticky tongues snaps up a butterfly. Then she smiled at him, now fully sated.

"Why you little…," David said.

Syd gave a little witch's laugh and said, "Sucker."

David couldn't help but laugh and decided he could love her more after all. On their drive back to their rented villa, he realized that leaving New York was the best decision they had ever made. They were both more relaxed, were enjoying the Italian way of life, and his writing had never been better. Something about getting rest, having great food, quality sex, and a few million dollars in the bank made for a pretty good life.

CHAPTER 69

ON THE DRIVE HOME FROM DINNER, a mile from their villa, David thought he saw the glint of a car following them. The car's headlights weren't on, but the full moon reflecting off the windows and chrome of the vehicle about a hundred yards behind them created brief glimmers of light that David could detect in his rearview mirror.

Not wanting to cause Syd any concern, he didn't mention the car. Instead he said, "Let's take a little ride; the moon is beautiful tonight."

David drove past their normal turnoff and picked up some speed along the narrow roadway bordered by low stone walls and Mediterranean cypress trees. Syd sat quietly in the passenger seat but gave a subtle tug on her seat belt.

As David slowly increased his speed over the uneven roadway, he could see the shadow of the vehicle trailing them keep pace. David slowed his speed and the car behind them backed off and remained a hundred yards behind.

David decided to quit screwing around. He downshifted the Porsche 930 S-4 and stabbed the accelerator. The car jumped from thirty miles per hour to over eighty in three seconds. As the S-Type continued to gather speed, the car in the rearview mirror was no longer visible.

At over one hundred miles per hour, David saw a sign for a four-way stop ahead. When he approached the intersection, he turned off his headlights, moved from sixth to second gear, slammed on the brakes, and made the ninety-degree turn with the help of a four-wheel drift maneuver he had learned in a driver's class for Porsche owners. He pulled off to the side of the road and slid behind the nearest low stone wall fifty yards from the intersection.

"Nice move, Mario. How far back are they?" Syd asked.

"We'll see."

From his position, David could still see the four-way stop behind him and within seconds he saw a dark Jaguar sedan flash through the rural intersection at ninety miles per hour. Fortunately for the car's occupants, there were no cars impeding its progress. Unfortunately for the car's occupants, a large oak tree adjacent to a slight bend in the road was.

David didn't see the impact, but he heard it and saw a flash of fire as the Jag exploded in an inferno that quickly enveloped the car, one of the two men in the car, and the four-hundred-year-old oak tree in which the Jag was now deeply embedded.

After several moments, David made a U-turn on the deserted road and drove to where the Jag now smoldered and billowed black smoke into a black sky. David and Syd got out of the Porsche and walked toward the Jag. They saw the driver who had already been turned to a black ember still strapped in his seat belt behind a charred air bag.

His passenger who was also very dead hung face-up out of the front passenger window while his lower torso was still enveloped in a low flickering flame. Syd walked up to the dead man and fully expected to see one of the men from the restaurant in the Jag. "This guy is not one of the guys…"

"I know, we need to get home, now," David said.

CHAPTER 70

BACK IN THE PORSCHE, DAVID made another quick U-turn and had the coupe at red line in seconds and within minutes pulled into the long winding driveway of their villa. David turned off the headlights as he neared the house and stopped before entering the courtyard when he saw an unfamiliar sedan near the front door. It was an Audi.

Without speaking, David and Syd exited the car at the same time and moved along a wooden fence that bordered the property. They stayed on the outside of the fence until they were in a position to see inside the old renovated farmhouse.

From their vantage point fifty feet from the kitchen window of the villa, they could see Syd's mother and the colonel as they sat at the kitchen table. There was a man sitting at the table with them and a second man standing next to Syd's father with something in his hand. They were the well-dressed men they had seen at the restaurant.

Using hand signals, Syd directed David to move around to the back door of the villa, while she indicated she would try the laundry room door. David nodded, pointed to his watch then raised then quickly opened and closed his hands three times before he moved into position. Syd nodded and ran to the door while she counted to thirty.

Within a second of each other, both had kicked down their respective doors and entered the villa amidst a cacophony of broken glass and fractured wood. When they arrived in the kitchen from different directions, Syd's mother calmly said, "That was a bit uncalled for, wasn't it?"

"Mom, Dad, are you guys okay!? Where are the kids!? And what the hell are you guys doing here!?" Syd asked in rapid-fire fashion not really giving anyone an opportunity to answer.

"Sydney, we are fine, the kids were asleep, although you guys probably just woke them up with that dramatic entrance of yours, my Lord, what were you two thinking? We were just having a nice conversation with these two gentlemen from the Office of Naval Intelligence, so calm down for heaven's sake."

With a coffee cup in his hand, one of the men who stood next to the table spoke. "Sydney, David, I am Captain Carl Burton, and this is Captain Robert Wells. We are with the European Division of ONI, which I know you guys are familiar with. Bob and I apologize for not introducing ourselves earlier tonight at dinner." Captain Burton looked at Syd's parents and asked, "Folks would you mind excusing us for a few minutes—we need to speak with Sydney and David privately."

"Of course," Sydney's mother said, "C'mon Henry, let's go check on the kids."

After Syd's parents left the room David said, "Captains, you are clearly following us, and I would like you to cut the crap and tell us why you are here."

"Actually, we are not the only people following you, David."

"If you mean the two guys in the Jag, you can find them about five clicks down the road resembling a British automotive barbeque."

"Are they dead?" Captain Wells asked.

"Hitting an oak tree head on at ninety tends to make people dead." David advised.

"Who were they and why were they after us?" Syd asked.

"They worked for Russian intelligence, and we have been tracking them tracking you for three months now. It actually started back in New York, and the surveillance moved here when you relocated."

"You didn't say why they were after us," Syd said.

"We're not quite sure. We picked up some intercepts from our New York office that related to David and his book, but we didn't get anything concrete other than they were keeping tabs on you guys. It really got our attention when they followed you guys over here and deployed two full-time assets to keep track of all your movements," Captain Burton explained.

"Are they linked with Connie Reynolds and her group?" David asked.

"Not that we can see," Captain Wells replied.

"Then why would the Russians be interested in me and my book? It wasn't me who accused them of messing with our elections. That was the House and Senate. Hell, everyone already knows their elections over there are rigged anyway, so it couldn't be that."

"We don't know what they're up to. All we do know is they have been on your tails for over three months. We also wanted to know why," Captain Burton explained.

"Captain, did I detect an accusatory tone in that question?" Syd asked.

"I would not say accusatory, Sydney, but it is fair to say we are curious why Russian assets would be tailing an American writer, his wife, and family. Do you folks have any idea why you were, and presumably are, still under surveillance? David, are you writing a new book about another issue about U.S. elections that could stir up interest from the Russians?"

"I am working on a story about baseball and Nazi Germany. The Russians are not even mentioned in either."

"You never really answered the question of why you are trailing us other than we were being trailed. Did you think we were in danger?" Syd asked.

"Not sure you are in danger. But not sure you aren't either. From the sounds of it, the guys in the Jag won't be telling us anything, but you can count on the fact they will be replaced within forty-eight hours. Look, you guys with your backgrounds know the score, if the Russians want to kill you, it's likely, even probable, you're going to end up dead. The only question is when," Captain Burton said flatly.

"If I am to get killed, I would at least like to know why. At least with Connie, I could understand why she wanted me dead. I have no idea why the Russians would want to kill me," David said.

"Well, not to pile on but it's also possible people from Connie's group will eventually come after you too. You riled up lots of folks with that book of yours. We have tracked down some of the online chatter, and most turned out to be fringe types talking tough. But there were some threats that we did take more seriously from some groups capable of carrying out some kind of retribution and there was some indirect linkage to some of Connie's alumni," Captain Wells said.

"Gee, nice to be so popular," David said.

"Probably best not to stay in any one place too long," Captain Burton advised.

"Well, we do like to travel," Syd said with a smile.

"That leads us to another reason we were trailing you guys, but it temporarily took a back seat when this Russian thing cropped up."

"You each want a signed copy of my book?" David asked.

"No, actually I read your book already and thought it was a bit far-fetched," Captain Wells said flatly.

"Fuck you," David said with a smile. A small smile.

Captain Burton continued, "The reason we were trailing you guys is we want both of you to come back into ONI and become assets for Naval Intelligence as you travel around the world selling your books."

Syd and David both laughed.

The two captains did not laugh.

"You're kidding, right?" David said.

"I don't think they are kidding," Syd said.

"Do we look like we're kidding?" Captain Wells asked.

David looked at the captains and concluded they did not look like they were kidding but he had to ask the obvious anyway. "Are you guys fucking kidding?"

"David, your book has created a great deal of worldwide interest in American politics, which will give you unlimited access to virtually every continent and a valid reason to frequently travel to innumerable countries. The fact that you and Sydney have military backgrounds and at one time had top-secret clearances makes you very viable assets if you would decide to return to a form of active, albeit clandestine, service," Captain Burton explained.

"You know, I always wanted to be a spy," Syd said in a voice that was almost a whisper.

"Yeah, I can see you as a female James Bond, carrying around a diaper bag, stuffed animals, baby wipes, and a two-seated stroller." David said.

"Actually, all that stuff is in fact pretty good cover, which makes you guys, at least for a couple years, people who could help us over here in Europe and even Asia," Captain Wells noted.

"What kind of spies are you looking for? We were both in the Navy but not Naval Intelligence. And how are we supposed to kill bad people if we can't find a babysitter?" David asked.

"I don't think you'll need to kill anybody, David, although from what I hear happened with those two guys who broke into your apartment, you can both take care of yourselves. All we would want you to do is look around at where you are. Take notes on things like possible changes in the public's attitude about a government or a specific leader. Try and get into the zeitgeist of the citizenry when you are at book signings, having dinners in restaurants, or talking to people in parks and stores. Just asking questions and getting answers from regular people can be extremely valuable to us," Captain Burton said.

"If Russian spies were trailing us here in Italy and could kill us at any time if they wanted to like you said, what kind of protection will we have if we are traveling all over the world? And what do we do with Gino and Marie? I am not going to leave my children alone and traipse all over the map just to give you guys a book report every month," Sydney said.

"We could easily give you two armed guards who could act as babysitters, au pairs, aides or whatever you want to call them, who would be with you at all times for your protection. That would be a logical and acceptable addition to your travel entourage in the eyes of the press and public."

"Would they be able to change diapers too?" David asked with a half-smile.

"Yes, I am quite certain we could arrange for that skill set," Captain Wells said solemnly.

"David, in some ways by traveling we do become more difficult to hit, you know, a moving target. If the Russians could find us, then maybe

Connie's group could too, eventually. What do you think?" Syd asked, still thinking of that female James Bond comparison.

"Are we going to get paid for this?" David asked bluntly.

"If you mean will you get rich coming back into the Navy, the answer is no," Captain Wells said.

"I don't want money. I want the Navy to buy 100,000 copies of each of my books for as long as we do our spy thing."

"What the hell would the Navy do with 100,000 copies of *STAT$*? Or with your other books?" Captain Burton asked.

"Donate them to libraries, give them away as Christmas presents, or burn them, I don't really care what you do with them. But if I'm going to travel all over the world as an author and spy guy, I want to do so on the *New York Times* best seller list. C'mon guys, just think of it as adding to our cover and to provide us better protection."

The captains were silent for several moments, glanced at each other, then nodded.

"That's a can-do affirmative," Captain Wells said.

"Great, just one more condition."

"What's that?" Captain Wells asked, not at all sure it would be the last condition.

"Can we select one of our own guards to watch over us while we are doing God's work over here?" David asked.

"As long as they pass our background checks and have some kind of experience in this area, I guess that could be arranged," Captain Wells said.

Sydney and David smiled at each other against the backdrop of two crying kids.

EPILOGUE

DAVID MADE A CALL AND got voice mail. "Hey Ernie, it's me, David Dawson. We took your advice and got out of Dodge and are now in Europe. I wanted to talk to you about an opportunity to travel and see the world that you might find interesting. Give me a call on this number, it's secure. We can discuss details. By the way, have you ever changed a diaper? Take care."

"Think he'll be interested?" Syd asked.

"Yeah, I do. He's still a Marine at heart, and he's one guy I would trust with our lives. I hope he's interested."

"What do you think of our first assignment?"

"A month in France can't be all bad, not with all the five-star hotels we'll be staying at. And don't forget the food. By the way, how many book signings did you say we had lined up?"

"Seventeen so far." Syd said after checking their itinerary on her iPad.

"When do we meet with our ambassador?"

"The sixteenth"

"Sounds like your mom and the colonel are psyched over this adventure."

"Yeah, the colonel is teaching both kids how to speak French."

"French? Marie can't even speak English yet."

"He wants them to be well-rounded."

"We'll be meeting them in Paris on Friday?" David asked.

"Yeah. Captain Wells has found an au pair who was in the British Special Forces. She knows Europe like the back of her hand and actually liked your book. She can break several concrete blocks with either foot and won the marksmanship award in her graduating class at her academy. She is also trained to handle several types of weapons. They will all take the train to Paris and meet us at the hotel around five on Friday."

"That's all good," David said. "You ready to go?"

"Yes, I am. I never knew being a mother could be this much fun."

After loading the Porsche in front of the repaired door of the farmhouse, David and Syd waved good-bye to her parents, Gino, Marie, and Captain Burton who was about to get a lesson from Syd's mom on the safest way to change a dirty diaper. He did not look amused.

The beginning.

ABOUT THE AUTHOR

FOR MARK DONAHUE, 30 years in senior management at two Fortune 200 firms was enough. So, he quit and decided, at long last, to write. The result was five novels released in 2020 and eleven screenplays, three of which are in pre-production as feature films. "Guess I should have left commercial real estate sooner." His readers wholeheartedly agree.

Mark resides in Ohio with wife Marsha, Mika, The Wonder Dog, and boss of the house, Rocky the Cat. Much missed, and immortalized in Mark's first novel, *Last at Bat*, the late great Wheaten Terrier Carly, watches over all of them from an honored perch on a bookshelf—where else would a writer's dog be?

www.DonahueLiteraryProperties.com

D!
DONAHUE
LITERARY PROPERTIES